BORIS PASTERNAK

Zhenia's Childhood

and other stories

ALLISON & BUSBY
LONDON · NEW YORK

First published in this edition 1982 by
Allison & Busby Ltd.
6a Noel Street
London W1V 3RB
and distributed in the USA 1982 by
Schocken Books Inc.
200 Madison Avenue
New York
NY 10016   18213655

This translation © Allison & Busby 1982
British Library Cataloguing in Publication Data
Pasternak, Boris
  Zhenia's childhood, and other stories
  I Title.
    891.73'44[F]   PG3476.P27
ISBN 0-85031-466-6
ISBN 0-85031-467-4-Pbk

The publishers wish to acknowledge the financial assistance of the Arts
Council of Great Britain.

Printed and bound in Great Britain by
The Camelot Press Ltd., Southampton

Contents

Zhenia's Childhood

THE LONG DAYS

I

SHE was born and grew up in Perm. Her most distant memories, like once her little ships and dolls, sank deep into shaggy bearskins; the house was full of them. Her father managed the Lunievski Mines and also had extensive connexions with the Chusova River mill-owners.

Gift bearskins were dark brown, deep-piled. The white she-bear in the nursery was like a huge bedraggled chrysanthemum. This was the bearskin specially acquired for 'our pet Zhenia's room'—she had taken a fancy to it, they at once went into the shop and bargained and bought it and a man delivered it.

They used to spend their summers in a chalet on the far side of the River Kama. In those years, Zhenia was put to bed early. She could not see the glow of the Motovilikha fires. But one day something frightened the Angora cat and it fidgeted in its sleep and woke Zhenia up. Then she saw there were grown-ups on the balcony. The alder which overhung the railing was as dense and scintillating as ink. The tea in the glasses was red. Cuffs and cards were yellow, the cloth green. Just like being delirious. Only this being delirious had a name. And Zhenia knew the name. It was *cards*.

On the other hand, it was absolutely beyond her to know what was going on far, far away, on the other bank. That had no name, nor had it got any definite colour or shape. When it got excited, it was all near and dear, not delirium like that muttering and twirling in the clouds of tobacco smoke, casting fresh, windy shadows on the yellowish timbers of the balcony.

1

And Zhenia burst into tears. Her father came in and explained. Her English governess turned her face to the wall. Her father's explanation was brief. That was Motovilikha that she could see. Such a big girlie. Hushabye. Girlie understood nothing, gratified swallowed a tear that rolled down. Because that was all she wanted: what the incomprehensible thing was *called*. It was called *Motovilikha*. And on this occasion that was the explanation of everything, because on this occasion a name still had a complete child-wise reassuring significance.

But when morning came, she began to ask questions about what Motovilikha was and what they did there in the night, and learned that Motovilikha was an ironworks, a government ironworks, and cast iron was made there and out of cast iron . . . But that did not interest her, what interested her was whether what they called ironworks were a special sort of tyrant-kings and who lived in them, but she did not ask anybody those questions. For some reason she deliberately kept them to herself.

This was the morning when she emerged from the babyhood in which she had still been during the night. For the first time in her life she sensed that there was some sort of phenomenon in what a phenomenon either kept to itself or, if it revealed it to anyone, revealed exclusively to grown-ups able to shout, punish, smoke and bolt doors. For the first time she became like her new Motovilikha. She did not say everything that came into her mind, but kept the most important, the essential and worrying part of it to herself.

The years rolled on. Ever since they were born the children had been so accustomed to their father's absences that in their eyes rarely eating dinner and never eating any supper became a special characteristic of fatherhood. But in that gravely empty, utterly vacant house more and more often there began to be dancing and fun and drinking and eating, but Zhenia's English governess's chilly teaching could never replace the presence of her mother, who filled the whole house with the sweetly oppressive atmosphere of her touchy temper and obstinacy, which was like a sort of electricity.

In through the curtains poured the quiet northern daylight.

That did not smile. The oak sideboard looked grey. The silver reared heavy and oppressive. Across the white cloth moved the lavender-washed hands of the governess. She never shared out wrong, she never lacked patience, and a sense of fair play was an essential part of her just as much as her bedroom was always clean and tidy and her books too.

When she had brought in the food the housemaid hung about in the dining-room; she did not go back to the kitchen till the time came to bring in another dish. All comfortable and very fine. But frightfully sad.

And since for Zhenia these were years of loneliness and suspicion and a sense of sin and what one wanted to call *christian-isme* in French since so much could never be called just 'christianity', it sometimes seemed to her that after all life could not possibly be any better, nor ought to be, because of her wickedness and the insufficiency of her repentance, so it all served her right. Whereas, though the children were never conscious of this, it was just the other way round, their whole inner life had been badly jolted, it was in ferment, they were completely baffled by their parents' relationship to them, whenever mamma and father were home, that is, when they came, not home, but back to the house.

Her father's rare moments of humour failed altogether and invariably missed the mark. He was aware of this and that too the children understood. His features invariably wore a sort of bloom of dismal embarrassment. Whenever he lost his temper he became a total stranger, yes, a stranger, and in the very instant when he began to lose control of himself. You don't have any feeling for strangers. The children never, never answered him back.

But for some time since the criticism coming from the nursery and, if unspoken, clear in the children's eyes, had found him quite insensitive. It was ist not noticed by him. Resistant to every such reagent, somehow unknowable, therefore pitiable, *this* father was terrible, quite the opposite of the lose-his-temper father—the stranger. His little daughter was more moved by *him* than his son was. But they were both troubled most of all by their mother.

3

Mother smothered them with caresses, mother was always giving them presents, and was always spending hours on end with them when they least of all wanted her to, for in such moments it was all such a burden to their child consciences because it was so unmerited, nor did they recognize themselves in the lavish petting names which her instinct was then wont to shower over them.

Hence often, when one of those rare moments of peace came into their souls in which they ceased to be aware of the criminal within them, when all that mysterious force which, just like the fever you had when measles were coming on, all that mysterious force which would take control protected them, their mother seemed alienated from them, as if she avoided them, getting irritable for no cause whatsoever. The postman came. The letter was given to the addressee, that is, to mamma, and they saw her take it without so much as a 'thank-you'.

"Go to your room," she says suddenly, to Zhenia. Bangs the door. And they both quietly hung their heads and felt so miserable, yes, for a long, long time felt so wretched and puzzled.

At first they used often to cry, then, after one particularly violent fit of temper, they began to be afraid, after which, as the years went by, it changed to a concealed dislike which took ever deeper root within them.

Anything that did pass from parents to children came their way adventitiously and inopportunely, not at all of their prompting, but for some quite unconnected reason, and was somehow remote, as things always are when clandestine, night hearts aching at the gates, with all the town abed.

.   .   .   .   .

Here was the ambience of the children's upbringing, though they knew nothing of it, because rare is the adult who knows, who hears what shapes him, makes him, knits him to be a human being. Life endows very few with awareness of what it does to them, too passionately it loves its creation and in its workings it speaks to none but some of those few who actively wish life success and love life's workshop. Nor is any person empowered to give aid, though any one may hinder. How can life be hindered? Like this: imbue a tree with concern for its own growth and it will grow weedy or be all stock or squander everything on one leaf, because it will have forgotten the universe, which should always be the example, and, producing something which is one of a thousand, it will make thousands of copies of one thing.

And to ensure against dead wood in the soul—to have no check to its growth, so man should not mix his stupidity in the planning of his immortal essence—there has been much instituted that distracts his frivolous curiosity from life, which does not like him to look on at its workings and in endless ways avoids him. It is to this end that all true religions, all general concepts and all the prejudices of men have been introduced, the most striking and most entertaining of these being psychology!

The children had now emerged from primal infancy. The concepts of punishment, requital, reward and justice had now in child fashion entered their souls, distracting their conscious minds, so that life might do to them what it felt was required, what was important, what was beautiful.

II

It was something Miss Hawthorn herself would never have done. But during one of her attacks of unprovoked sentimentality towards the children, Mrs Lüvers over the merest trifle gave the English governess more than a little tongue-pie. And that was the end of the governess. Soon after, without anybody really noticing, a curious, weedy Frenchwoman sprouted in her place. Later all that Zhenia could recall was that this Frenchwoman resembled a fly and nobody liked her. Her name was lost for ever, nor could Zhenia even give a hint among what syllables or sounds it might be found. All she could recall was that, first, the Frenchwoman shouted at her, then she took a pair of scissors and snipped and sheared the patch of the bearskin which was bloodstained off short.

Zhenia had the impression that now people would always shout at her and her headache would never stop, it would always be with her, and she would never more be able to understand that page in her favourite book, it just all swam together in front of her eyes like any lesson-book after dinner.

The day dragged on endlessly. Her mother was out. She was not sorry about that. She even thought she was pleased.

Very soon, however, the long day was consigned to oblivion, somewhere among the French past and future anterior tenses, giving the hyacinths their watering and going for a walk along Sibirskaya and Okhanskaya Streets. The day was indeed so completely forgotten that the longness of another long day, the second in order in her life, only struck her and was felt by her in the early evening, while she was reading by lamplight and the slow-moving story was giving rise to hundreds of most trivial reflections.

When later she called to mind that house in Osinskaya Street where they were living at the time, it always figured in her imagination exactly as she saw it just as the light was fading on that second long day. It had really been a very long day. Outside it was Spring. In the Urals Spring is weedy, slow to come to fruition, then all at once it breaks out all over the place, noisily, in a mere night, and after that never ceases to be all over the place and noisy. The lamps with their shadows merely marked off the emptiness of the evening air. They gave out no light, merely swelled from inside, like diseased fruit, suffering from a dropsy, at the same time cloudy and clear, which expanded their puffy shades. Themselves absent. Falling into their proper places on the tables, coming down from the ceiling plaster in the rooms in which she had grown accustomed to seeing them. Yet the contact between those lamps and the rooms was far less than their contact with the Spring sky. They seemed to be held up close into that, like glasses of water to somebody ill in bed. At heart Zhenia was out in the street where the servants' chatter teemed and the drip-a-drip grew thinner as it froze up for the night. That was where the lamps vanished in the evening. Her parents were away, though it seems that her mother was expected back that very day. That long day, or very soon after. Yes, probably. Or she may have turned up unexpectedly. Perhaps that was it.

She was beginning to get into bed when she noticed that the day had been long for the same reason that the other one had, and her first thought was to get the scissors and cut out those patches in her nightgown and the bed-sheet. Then she decided to take the Frenchwoman's face-powder and rub that in white. And she had just taken the powder-box when in came the Frenchwoman and smacked her. It was of course the powder that made the sin. Powdering herself! The idea! The last straw! Now at last the governess understood. She had had her eye on this for some time.

Zhenia cried because of the smacking, because of the nagging and from wounded sensitivity, because, though she felt innocent of what the Frenchwoman suspected her of, she knew something about herself which—and this she could *feel*—was far more beastly than what she was suspected of. She must—this she felt persistently till she could feel nothing else at all, felt it in her calves and her temples—this, no matter how, this at all cost, she knew, though neither for what reason or to what end, she must hide. Dully aching, all her joints fused into one mesmeric insistence, exhausting her, wearing her out. That insistence was part of her very flesh, concealing the sense of it all from the child, and by making her behave like a criminal made her conclude the bleeding to be some revolting and beastly sort of evil.

"Menteuse!" cried the governess. "Liar!" All she could do was go on saying *"No"*, stubbornly shutting herself away in the most loathsome of all states, somewhere between the disgrace of illiteracy and the shame of a street quarrel. Had to hug herself to the wall, trembling, gritting her teeth, but letting the tears flow. She could not go and fling herself in the river, because it was still cold outside and the Kama was full of the last floes.

Neither Zhenia herself nor the Frenchwoman heard the doorbell in time. The hullabaloo the two of them were making had

soaked so deep into the dark brown bearskins, and when her
mother came into the room it was already too late, she found
her little daughter in tears and the Frenchwoman scarlet with
rage. She demanded an explanation. The Frenchwoman told
her straight that—no, not Zhenia, no, 'your child'!—'your
child' used powder, she had in fact noticed it previously and—
but mother did not let her finish—her horror was not put on—
Zhenia was not even thirteen.

"Zhenia! You? Oh dear Heaven, whatever are we coming to?"

In that moment her mother thought such language fitting,
to make out she had already been aware that her daughter was
beginning to be badly behaved and getting into shocking
habits, and it was all her fault for not taking steps earlier;
now see to what depths her Zhenia had sunk!

"Zhenia," she said, "now tell me the whole truth or it will
be so much the worse! What were you doing . . . ?"

'*With that powder-box*' no doubt Mrs Lüvers intended to
say. But she said "*with this thing*" and, grabbing the '*thing*',
waved it about.

"Mamma, don't you believe Mamzel, I never did . . ."

And she burst out sobbing. And in those sobs her mother
could hear ominous sounds which were not there at all, and she
felt she was guilty and inwardly was horrified by herself,
thought she must now put everything right, and, even if it
was all against her maternal instincts, must 'rise to the neces-
sary level of decency and child-upbringing', and she resolved
not to be moved at all by sympathy, merely to wait till that
flood of heartrending tears dried up.

And she sat down on the bed, gazing calmly and vacantly
at the end of the bookshelf. It smelt of expensive scent. When
her little girl came to herself again, she once more began to
cross-examine her. Zhenia shot one glance up at the window
and, before her eyes were properly dry, there she was sobbing
again. The ice-man was coming, it must be the ice-man
making that noise. A star twinkled. So cold and so malleable,
the never-ebbing empty night rustled, blackly. Zhenia looked
away from the window. There was now an undertone of impatience in her mother's voice, while her French governess stood

by the wall, the embodiment of gravity and concentrated educational principles, her hand, like that of a junior officer with his general, resting on her watch ribbon. Again Zhenia looked out at the river and the stars. Her mind was at last made up. Despite the cold and the floes. And—she plunged.

Tongue-tied, terror-stricken, beside herself, she told her mother about *it*. Her mother let her go on to the very end solely because she was so struck by the emotion the child put into her communication. For she had of course guessed the truth from the first few words. Not even the words—the tremendous gulp the child gave before she began. So she heard her out, so glad, loving her so, faint from her fondness for the dear little mite. With an urge all the time to fling her arms round her daughter's neck and burst into tears herself. But there were always those educational principles, so, getting up from the bed, she snatched away the coverlet, then called her daughter to her and, stroking her little head so slowly, so slowly, so caressingly, said what a good girl she was. The words broke quickly from her, then noisily she strode to the window, turning away from Zhenia and her governess.

Zhenia could not see her French governess at all. The tears were transfixed. So was her mother, the whole room.

"Who makes the bed?"

Senseless question. The little girl shuddered. She was sorry for Grusha, the maid. Then, in French, Zhenia recognized it but did not recognize the words, something was said; stern expressions, too. Then, again to her, in quite a different voice:

"Zhenia, my pet, go into the dining-room a moment, will you, dearie. I'll be with you in a moment. I want to tell you all about the lovely chalet we've hired for you—for us, next summer."

The lamps were themselves again, just as they were in the winter, at home at the Lüvers', warm lamps, hearty, loyal. Across the blue table-cloth lay Mummy's frisky marten necktie.

Case won staying on over holiday wait till end holy week if . . .

The remainder was illegible, the telegram was folded at the corner. Tired and happy, Zhenia sat down on the edge of the sofa. Sat modestly, nicely, exactly as she sat half a year later, six months later, in the corridor of the Ekaterinburg Lycée, on the end of a cold, yellow bench, when she got full marks for her answers in Russian oral and was told she 'might go'.

. . . . .

The next morning her mother explained what she must do whenever it happened, it was nothing to worry about, it would happen often. She did not give anything a name or explain anything, though she did add that from now on she would be her little girl's teacher, as she was not going away any more. And the French governess was dismissed for her inattentiveness, after having been with them some months. When the driver came to take her away and she was going down the stairs, on the landing she met the doctor on his way up and he did not even say *good-bye*. She guessed that he must know all about it. She frowned and shrugged her shoulders.

At the front door was the housemaid who had answered it to the doctor, and afterwards, in the hall, where Zhenia was, the sound of footsteps and echoing stone lingered longer than it should. Thus her memory of how her first period happened was stamped with the sonority of the morning street all a-chatter sweeping fresh into the house and lingering on the stairs, with that French governess, the housemaid and the doctor, equal to two criminals and one initiate, all bathed in light and the chill air and the sonority of noisy feet marching and disarmed by it all.

. . . . .

It was April, warm and sunny. '. . . *your feet, wipe your feet* . . .' rang the bare, bright corridor, from end to end. The bearskins put away for the summer. Each room at morning rising clean, transformed, with sweet sighs of relief. All day, all the wearisomely, never-setting, endlessly bogged-in day, in

every corner of all the rooms, over the window-panes leant
against the walls, in the mirrors, in vodka glasses of water and
in the blue atmosphere of the garden, never enough, never
quenched, with twinkling radiant countenance laughed and
danced the wild cherry blossom and the honeysuckle caught
its breath and bubbled. For a whole day and night now there
had been that tiresome chatter of the courtyards, throughout
the livelong day with tinkling tiny voices declaring night
overthrown, and from time to time welled loud like decoctions
of sunlight declaring that evenings were all abolished now
and there would be no more sleeping.

'Your feet, your feet!'

But those feet were hot with speed, coming in bacchanalian
from the outer air, with ringing in the ears, whereby they
could not clearly catch anything that was said, but rushed into
the dining-room at top speed to gulp and to gobble, then with
a clatter of thrust-back chairs to race out again into that day,
soaring free-breaking beyond supper, where the drying tree
gave out its brittle sound and the blue sky shrieked its whispered secret and the soil gleamed richly as if all melted down.
The borderline 'twixt house and outer air worn thin. Floors,
creaking floors, the polish gleaming dry, never all wiped clean.

Her father had brought dainties and wonders. The whole
house was wonderfully happy. Stones with dewy rustle fore-
warned of their emergence from many-hued cigarette paper,
ever and ever more transparent, layer after layer, white and
soft as lint, as those parcels were undone. Some were like drops
of milk of almonds, others—splashes of sky-blue water-colour,
yet others—congealed tears of cheese. These were blind, sleepy,
pensive, these others, with dancing sparks, the frozen juice of
blood oranges. One was afraid even to touch them. They were
so fine on that paper foam which extruded them as a ripe
plum its sultry nectar.

Father was now unusually kind to the children and often
took mother into town. And they would return together, and
seemed so happy. But what was most important was that they
were both so calm, both in the same mood, and both so easy
and kind, and when sometimes mother stole a glance at him

11

with a whimsical scolding word it looked just as if she dipped into his eyes, which were small and ugly, and scooped peace out of them, to pour it out again with her own, so big and so lovely, all over the children and everybody else.

On one occasion her parents got up very late. Later, Zhenia had no idea why, they decided to have dinner on a steamer moored in the harbour and they took the children with them. They let Seriozha try a sip of iced beer. They all enjoyed it so that they went to lunch on a steamer another time. The children found their parents unrecognizable. Whatever had come over them? The little girl lived in uncomprehending bliss, it seemed to her life would be like that now for ever and ever. They were not at all sad when they were told that this summer they were not being taken to a chalet. Their father went away soon after that. Three travelling chests appeared in the house. They were huge, yellow chests with stout iron bands round them.

III

The train left late at night. Mr Lüvers had gone a month ahead, and now wrote that the flat was ready. A lot of cabs went rattling down to the station. You could see when the station was near by the colour of the cobbles. They turned black and the street lamps looked like rusty iron. At the same time there was suddenly a view of the Kama, from a viaduct, where beneath them a gulf ran thundering out, black as soot, all heavy weights and clatter. The gulf shot away like an arrow into the far distance where it took fright, unrolling and all a-tremble with the twinkling tiny beads of signalling distances.

It was windy. The outlines flew off the hutments and fencing like the frames flying off sieves, flickering and flapping in the tattered air, and there was a smell of boiled potatoes. Their driver pulled out of the succession of basket trunks and bobbing up and down hindquarters and began to overtake them all. They recognized the wagon with their own luggage a long way off. When they drew level, from the driver's seat Ouliasha yelled something to her mistress, but the clatter of the wheels drowned the words. She went on bobbing up and down in her seat, her voice bobbed up and down too.

The little girl did not notice any sadness because of the novelty of all these night noises and the blacknesses and the freshness. Far, far ahead something loomed black that she could not make out. Beyond the harbour buildings little lights were swaying as the town plucked them off the river bank and off the boats and dipped them in the water. Then there were suddenly such a lot of them, all thick packed, blind, like maggots. In the Liubimovsky docks the funnels and the warehouse roofs and the decks showed blue and there were barges sprawling there, staring up at the stars.

'This place is a rat warren,' Zhenia said to herself.

All round them were the white stevedores. Seriozha jumped down first. He looked all round him and was most surprised when he saw that the truck with their luggage was also there—the horse raised its muzzle, the muzzle turned into a trunk, the horse reared on its hind legs like a barn-door cock, heaved its hindquarters against the truck and the truck moved back. All the way his one thought had been how much they would be left behind! And he stood now in his neat little white schoolboy's tunic, suddenly completely absorbed by the nearness of their journey. The journey was a novelty for them both. But he already knew—and loved—the words: *warehouse, locomotives, sidings, through-coach.* And the sound of the word *class* was sour-sweet to him. His sister was interested in all this too, but in her own way, without the boyish system which distinguished her brother's enthusiasm.

All at once there was their mother, at their very side, springing out of the ground. Orders were given to take the children to the restaurant. And when they got there, there she was again, making her way through the crowd, floating proudly like a peahen, and made straight for the person who, for the first time in the great outer world, they heard called by that sonorous and impressive title: *station-master.* How often they were to hear it later, in how many places, in how many forms, and amid all sorts of crowds!

Overcome by yawns, they sat for a long time at one of the

windows. The windows were all so dusty, so clumsy and so big that they seemed like institutions made of bottle glass in which you had to take your hat off. And now the little girl saw that on the far side of the window there was no street at all, instead, there was another room, only it was a more serious, more dismal room than this one inside the glass bottle. Into that room came locomotives. They crept in very slowly, then they came to a stop and made everything dark. When they went away again, emptying the room, it did not look like a room at all, because you could see the sky beyond some slender pillars, and beyond the sky a hill and some wooden houses, and everybody was making his way in that direction, afar off. Perhaps the cock birds were crowing there now, and there was a water-tank and it made a frightful mess. . . .

This was a country railway station. There was none of the confusion or the glow of a big city station; all its people collected in good time, coming out of the town by night, not just to travel, but also to have a long wait—a station with peace and quiet in it and people migrating to other parts, who slept about on the floor with gun-dogs and wooden travelling chests and machines sewn into tarpaulins and bicycles stark naked.

They went to bed in the top bunk. The boy fell asleep at once. And still the train had not started. It was beginning to get light, and little by little it became clear to the little girl that the railway coach was blue, clean and cool . . . gradually it became clear to her. . . . But then she was already asleep, too.

.   .   .   .   .

It was a very stout man. He was reading a newspaper. And jolting. When you looked at him you became aware of that jolting with which everything in the compartment was soaked and splashed as it was with the sunshine. From above Zhenia examined the man with that leisurely, detailed examination with which one thinks about anything or looks at anything when one has quite wakened up and is quite fresh and merely staying in bed because one is waiting for the decision to get up to come all by itself, clear and unforced, without any help like one's other thoughts. She examined him and wondered wherever he had come from and why he was in the compartment with them and however he had found the time to get washed and dressed? She had no notion what the time really was. She had just wakened up, therefore it was morning. She examined the man, but he could not examine her. Her bunk sloped right back to the wall. He could not see her also because, on account of the news, he very rarely looked up or down or to either side, but even when he did raise his eyes towards her bunk, their glances did not meet, he either saw only the mattress or else . . . but here, very quickly, she tucked them in under her and pulled her stockings up tight; they were coming down. Mamma was in the corner underneath. She was properly dressed and reading a book. So Zhenia decided by reflection while she studied the fat man. But there was no sign of Seriozha, even down below. So wherever could he be? She relaxed into a glorious yawn and stretched. It was terribly hot. That she only now realized, peering over her head at the window, which was half down.

'But wherever is the ground?' she suddenly wondered, with alarm.

What she saw was indescribable. The noisy hazel wood into which their train had thrust like a snake had become an ocean, a world, anything, everything. Dazzling, rolling away down a slope, it raced past, far-flung and steep-falling, till afar off it became tiny and close-packed and hazy where it broke away straight down, there turning quite black, while what was suspended in the space beyond the gulf was like an enormous, wondrous thundercloud, all curls and whorls of blazing green, and this stood absolutely still, like stone, and was lost in thought. Zhenia held her breath. She felt immediately how swift was that carefree, utterly carried-away air, and it was at once clear to her that that thundercloud was some special sort of country or place with a reverberating mountainous name which cannonaded all round with the rocks and the sand which were cast down to the valley below, and it was only the hazel wood that knew this, whispering and whispering it, here and there and far, far away beyond, only the hazel wood.

And she leant over and asked the whole compartment:
"Is that—the Ural Mountains?"

. . . . .

All the rest of the journey she spent glued to the corridor
window. She took root at it and she kept sticking her head out.
Greedy for it all. She had discovered that it was nicer looking
back than ahead. Grandiose acquaintances receded into the
mists. After brief separation from them, while you sought them
out again, with precipitous rumble and rattling of chains which
sent a wave of icy air over the nape of your neck and then they
produced a new wonder right under your nose! The alpine
panorama parted to either side, and everything grew taller
and vaster. Some became black, others became brighter, some
obscured themselves, others obscured yet others as they came
together and separated again, going down to the depths, and
rising again.

All this took place in a slow, slow revolution, like the
circumambulation of the stars, with all the cautious restraint
of things gigantic, ever within a hair's breadth of catastrophe,
yet ever ensuring that the world was quite intact. And all these
complex transpositions were directed by a tremendous, never
fluctuating booming which the human ear could never hear,
but which saw everything. Gloomy and taciturn, that booming
swept them all with its eagle eye and inspected their grand
parade. That was how the Ural Mountains were organized,
mile after mile of them, and then reorganized.

Squinting because of the brilliant light, she went back into
the compartment for a moment. Mamma was talking to the
strange gentleman. She was laughing. Seriozha was swinging
about on the red plush from a leather belt fastened to the wall.
Mamma spat out the last stone into her palm, shook fallen
crumbs off her dress, then, bending down with swift and
nimble ease, tucked all the rubbish away under the seat.

Contrary to expectation, the stout gentleman had a husky,
pipy little voice, and clearly suffered from shortness of breath.
Mamma introduced him to Zhenia and gave her a mandarin.

16

He was a comical man, no doubt kind too, and when he talked he kept putting his chubby hand up to his mouth. Whatever he said swelled up big, but was always being suddenly interrupted and washed away. It seemed that he really came from Ekaterinburg, he had travelled all over the Urals and he knew that country very well, and when he produced a gold watch from his waistcoat pocket and put it right up against his nose, then tucked it back into his pocket again, Zhenia noticed what kind fingers he had. Like all fat people, he took things as if he were giving and his hand was always sighing, just as if he were offering it to be kissed, and it bounced softly, like a rubber ball on the floor.

"Not long now," he suddenly drawled. He squinted and talked out of the side of his mouth, sideways from the boy, though it was to him he was talking, then he puffed out his lips.

"Do you know there's a post," Seriozha interrupted, slipping down from the seat and running out into the corridor. "That's what they say. There's a post where Asia and Europe meet. And it's got ASIA written upon it!"

Zhenia simply did not understand, but when the fat man had explained to her what it was all about, she too ran to the same side of the train, to wait for that post, all afraid they had already slipped past it. In her enchanted brain *'where Asia and Europe meet'* rose up in the form of a strange, phantasmagoric barrier, no doubt like those iron bars which were put between people and the puma cage—a barrier of terrible, foul-smelling dangerousness, as black as midnight. She awaited that post as if it were the raising of the curtain on the first act of a tragedy of geography of which she had heard stories from onlookers and proud too and excited to be in on it and soon about to see it for herself.

Meanwhile the wonder which previously to this had prompted her to join the grown-ups in the compartment, continued monotonously, till it looked as if there never would be an end to the grey alder forest through which half an hour earlier the railroad had begun to make its way and nature just made no preparation at all for what was about to happen to it. And

17

Zhenia got quite annoyed with dull, dusty old Europe'for so clumsily postponing the commencement of the wonder. Then how put out she was when, as if in answer to a wild shriek from Seriozha, something rather like a tombstone flashed by the window. It turned sideways to them and then ran away, bearing that long-awaited fabulous legend away with it, deep into the alder, as it ran away from the alder tree which was pursuing it. In the same instant, as if by pre-arrangement, countless heads were thrust out of the windows of all classes and the train rushing down the slope in a cloud of dust came to new life, and Asia already had dozens of lanes to its credit. But there were still kerchiefs fluttering from flying heads and men exchanging glances and some were clean-shaven and some were bearded and they all flew on in clouds of whirling sand, flying and flying on still past the same dusty alders which so recently were European but now were all so very Asian.

IV

A new life began. Milk was not brought round to the kitchen door by a milk-woman, but fetched by Ouliasha, and she carried it in a pair of earthenware crocks, too, and there were special rolls, not like the rolls in Perm at all. Here the sidewalks were something between marble and alabaster, all polished watery shiny. Even in the shade the flagstones dazzled, they were like icy suns, and they thirstily absorbed the shadows of the neighbouring trees, which melted away on them, getting quite watery and thin. Here it was also quite different going out and about, the streets were broad and bright, with flower beds, 'like Paris,' Zhenia said, copying her father.

He said so the very day they arrived. It was all very lovely and spacious. Father had had something to eat before coming to the station and did not dine with them. His knife, fork and spoon stayed as clean and bright as Ekaterinburg was. He merely undid his napkin, then he lolled sideways, telling them about things. He unbuttoned his waistcoat and his shirt-front stuck out so fresh and powerful. He told them that this was a lovely European town and rang a bell when they were to clear empty plates away and bring some more food and he kept on ringing and talking. And by unknown passages from rooms to Zhenia still unknown a white maid came silently in, all starchy-crinkly white and black too, and they spoke to her in the plural and said 'you' to her, and though new she smiled at the mistress and the children as if they already knew each other. And she was given some instructions about Ouliasha, who was out there in the unfamiliar and probably very, very dark kitchen where no doubt there was a window out of which you could see something new, a church tower perhaps, or a street or some birds. And no doubt Ouliasha was there at this very minute asking that young lady the maid questions and putting on some of her old clothes ready to unpack later, asking questions and settling in and looking to see what corner the stove was in, whether it was in the same corner as in Perm or in some other corner.

The boy learned from his father that it was not far to walk to the lycée, it was quite near, and they must have seen it when they drove past. Father drank some Caucasian mineral water and when he had gulped it down he went on:

"Didn't I show you? Well, you can't see it from here. But perhaps you can from the kitchen," he added reflectively, "though no more than the roof."

Then he drank some more *Narzan* water and rang the bell.

The kitchen turned out to be bright, fresh, exactly—so it seemed a minute later—like what she had guessed it would be in the dining-room, with all she had imagined, a hearth of white and pale blue tiles, and two windows just as she had thought there would be. Ouliasha wrapped something round her bare arms, the room filled full with children's voices, there were men on the lycée roof and the top of scaffold poles sticking over it.

"Yes, it's being repaired," her father said, when, jostling each other and making a great noise, they all went back to the dining-room, by the corridor too, which now she knew though she did not yet know it well, but would have to explore it properly tomorrow, when she got out her exercise books and

19

had hung her glove-flannel up by its loop, in short, when she had finished the thousand-and-one things she had to do.

"Ex-quisite butter," her mother said, as she sat down, and they went to the schoolroom, which they had been to see before they took their fur caps off, as soon as they arrived.

"What makes this Asia?" she wondered, out loud.

But for some reason Seriozha just did not understand the question, which it was certain sure he would have understood at any other time. Till now he and she had shared everything. But now he rolled across to a map which was hanging on the wall and just swept one hand from top to bottom down the 'Ural Mountain Range', then shot her a glance, assuming her to be absolutely crushed by that argument.

To her mind suddenly came that event which had happened at noon. It was already so far away. It was quite impossible to credit that the day which contained all that was the same day that was 'today in Ekaterinburg' and still was, not all of it yet, of course, there was still more to come. But when she reflected that all that had slipped away behind her, in all its stupendous shape, into an appointed distance of its own, she experienced a sense of amazing spiritual exhaustion, the sort of exhaustion that her body felt as evening dragged on after a day of great effort. It was just as if she herself had taken part in the discovery and moving into place of those oh-so-heavy but lovely things and had strained herself. And being for some reason convinced that *they*, her Ural Mountains, were *there*, she spun round and raced away through the dining-room into the kitchen, where there was now less crockery, though that ex-quisite butter was still there with the ice on maple leaves all beady with sweat, and so was the angry mineral water.

The lycée was being done out, and the air was torn by strident swifts just like dressmakers tearing madapollam with their teeth and down below—she had stuck her head out— there was a gleaming carriage at an open stable door and sparks flying from a grindstone and the smell of all they had had for dinner, and it was better and more interesting than when it was served and it smelt melancholy for a long time like in a book. She had forgotten now what she had come here for and

20

did not notice that her Urals were not in Ekaterinburg, but
what she did notice was how gradually it grew dark in
Ekaterinburg, taking objects sedately one by one, and beneath
them workpeople were singing; it must be very light work, no
doubt they had washed the floor now, and were rolling the mats
into position with their hot hands and they just tipped out the
water from the washing-up bowl and although they sloshed it
down like that it was so quiet all round! She noticed too how
the water-tap gurgled, and how 'See, Miss'—but she was still
shy of the wonderful new maid and did not mean to pay any
attention to her, and she noticed—she did try to think her
thought out to the very end—that down beneath them people
knew and no doubt were saying:

"See, that's the new folk come to number two."

Ouliasha came into the kitchen.

The children slept soundly this first night, and Seriozha
woke up in Ekaterinburg, but Zhenia woke up in Asia, so it
seemed to her, again so wide and so strange. On the ceiling
freshly danced the flaky alabaster.

.   .   .   .   .

It had begun in the summer. She was suddenly notified that
she would go to the lycée. That was all that was delightful.
But they notified her. She did not ask her teacher to come to
the schoolroom, where the hues of the sunshine stuck so firmly
to the walls with their glue-paint wash that it was only with
blood that the evening could tear off the past day, it stuck so.
She had not asked him, but in he came, together with mamma,
to meet 'his future pupil'. She did not give him that ugly
surname Dikikh. And was it ever her wish that from now on
there were always soldiers drilling at midday, all stiff and
greedy and sweaty, like the red water-hammer of the tap when
something was wrong with the pipes, or for their boots to be
absolutely crushed by the purple storm-cloud which knew all
about guns and wheels, so much more than their white shirts
and white handkerchiefs and whitest of officers?

And was it by any request of hers that now invariably two

things—a plate and a table napkin—coming into contact, like the carbon pencils in an arc-lamp, should immediately cause a third thing which tended to dematerialize: the notion of death, like that sign hanging out at the barber's, where this first happened to her. And was it with her consent that those barricades 'prohibiting loitering' should become the scene of certain town secrets which against all the regulations did loiter, or that the Chinese should become personally frightful, her very own, and terrible?

Of course, she did not take everything so heavily to heart. Quite a lot, such as her forthcoming going to the lycée, was pleasant. But, just like going to the lycée, all the rest of it was all *notified*. Life had ceased to be a poetic trifle, it had plunged into a stern, sombre fable insomuch as it became prose and fact. And the elements of everyday existence made a sullen, a painful, a sombre impact on that soul which was thus getting involved in life, and it was just as if she were for ever turning from intoxication to a sober state.

All these things sank at once to the bottom of her soul, real things, things hardened off, things chill like sleepy leaden spoons. And there, at the very bottom, that lead began to float about, and it ran into little clots, dripping out in ideas that haunted her.

V

Some Belgians became frequent visitors at tea-time. That was what they were called—'the Belgians'. That was what her father called them. He would say: "The Belgians are coming round today." There were four of them. The one without any whiskers did not come very often. He was not talkative. Sometimes he came alone, just dropping in, on weekdays, always choosing bad, rainy weather. The other three were inseparables. Their faces were like cakes of fresh soap, soap not started, soap straight out of its wrappings, sweet-scented and chill. One had a beard which was thick and tufty and he also had tufty chestnut hair. They invariably came with her father, straight from some sort of 'meeting'.

The whole household was fond of them. They talked as if they were pouring water on the tablecloth, noisily, freshly, suddenly, and somehow all to one side, where nobody expected it to be, and you could always hear the consequences of their jokes and stories a long time after, they were always comprehensible to the children, always thirst-quenching and clean.

The din collected all round, the sugar-bowl gleamed, the nickel-plated coffee-jug, the clean white teeth, the solid linen. They would banter politely and graciously with mamma. Colleagues of her father, they possessed a subtle ability to restrain him just in time when in response to some frivolous hint of theirs or allusion to business or to personalities which only they among the company at table understood, her father ponderously, in not at all the best French, began a lengthy, stumbling story about counter-agents and *références approuvées*, and about *férocités*, that is to say, *bestialités, ce qui veut dire en Russe*—which in Russian meant kidnapping during Holy Week.

The one without any whiskers, who latterly had started learning Russian, often tested himself out in that new field, but he still did not catch on. It was hardly seemly to laugh at her father's French, indeed, they found all his *férocités* very tiresome, but the matter seemed to be put right by the laughter which Negarat's attempts produced.

That was his name—Negarat. He was a Walloon from the Flemish part of Belgium. Introduced by Dikikh. He had noted his address down in Russian, and he made the complicated letters, such as ю, Я and ѣ very funnily. They always turned out somehow double, straggling, splitting in two. The children took the liberty of kneeling on the leather armchair cushions and putting their elbows on the table. Everything indeed became permissible, everything got mixed up, ю was not ю, but a sort of ю, the whole company round the table roared and chortled, Evans banging the table with his fist and wiping away the tears, her father shaking with laughter and pacing up and down the room, crumpling his handkerchief, red-faced and declaring that no, this was really too much.

"*Faites de nouveau,*" Evans egged him on. "*Commencez.*"

But Negarat hesitated, just like a little rabbit, gaping there, puzzling out however he was going to get to know that Russian ы, as dark and obscure a region of the world as any colony of the Congo.

"*Dites les mots: ' ouvoui, nevouigodno',*" said her father, in a choking voice, quite hoarse, "Say in Russian, 'I'm very sorry, it's awkward'."

"*Ouvoui niévoui . . .*" the Belgian began.

"Do you hear that? Isn't it delightful?"

And they all mimicked him and all roared with laughter.

.　　　.　　　.　　　.　　　.

The summer passed. The examinations were taken and she had passed, some subjects with distinction. The chilly, transparent noise of the corridors streamed away like water out of a spring. Here everybody knew everybody. The leaves in the garden were turning yellow and gold. The classroom window-panes were dimmed by that bright, dancing reflection. Frosted half-way, they grew misty, and the lower part trembled. A bluish shudder ran through the casements. Their icy clarity was furrowed by the bronze twigs of the maples.

She had never realized that all her anxieties were going to be transformed into such a funny thing as that! *Divide such and such a number into* arshins 7! Now, was it really worth going through all the measures just for that? All those grammes and drachmas and scruples and ounces, which had always seemed to her to be the four quarters of the scorpion. Why should one have to use 'e' when one wrote *polezny* (useful), why 'e' and not that 'ѣ'? She only tried to give an answer because her whole mind concentrated on the effort to conceive such unsatisfactory reasons, by reason of which such a thing as a word *polѣzny* could ever exist at all, it looked so essentially funny and so shaggy too when one outlined it like that.

And she never did know why even so she was not sent to the lycée after all, despite being accepted and entered in the register, and her coffee-coloured uniform already being made and she even having a fitting with pins, so tiresome that was and lasted so long too, and in her room new horizons forming, such as her satchel, her pen-case, her luncheon basket, and a really horrible photograph of herself.

THE STRANGER

I

THE little Tartar girl was wrapped from head to knees in a thick woollen shawl and kept trotting about the yard like a tiny hen. Zhenia felt she would like to go and talk to that little Tartar girl. At which moment the shutters of the little window banged open and Axinia called "Nickie!" The child, like a peasant's bundle with felt slippers roughly stuffed into the bottom, toddled quickly over to the *concierge*'s little quarters.

Taking work outdoors always meant blunting any foot-note to a rule till it lost all sense and then going upstairs to begin all over again indoors. Indoors, as soon as you crossed the threshold, took possession of you with a special kind of gloom and coolness; there was always a special kind of quiet, unexpected familiarity, as if there each piece of furniture stood in a place that was allotted to it for all time. Nobody could foretell the future. But you could *see* it when you passed from the open inside; its plan was at once clear—that disposition to which, for all its unsubmissiveness in every other respect, it was bound to submit. And there was never a dream, wafted by the stir of the outer air, but that cheerful, decisive spirit of the house quickly shook it off the moment she entered the hall.

This time it was Lermontov. Zhenia crumpled the little volume, covers folded inside. Indoors if her brother Seriozha had done that she would have been the first to attack such a 'disgusting habit'. Outside it was different.

Prokhor put the ice-cream machine down and went back into the house. When he opened the door of the Spitzyns' flat

the infernal yelping of the General's hairless little puppies came
gambolling out. Then the door banged to with a sharp clang.

But the river Terek, lioness-like leaping, with that shaggy
mane on her back, still roared away, as appointed, only Zhenia
suddenly became a prey to doubts whether all that took place
on the Terek's back or on its neck. She was too lazy to check
it in the book, and the golden clouds from southern countries,
from afar, had scarcely managed to guide the poet to the
north, when there they were meeting her at the door of General
Spitzyn's kitchen, with a bucket and mop in their hands.

The batman put down the bucket and bent down, took the
ice-cream machine to pieces, and set about washing it. The
August sun brushed its way past the foliage of the trees and fell
on the batman's rump; it settled red in the faded army cloth
and soaked into it like turpentine.

The courtyard was large with all sorts of odd corners. A
courtyard both whimsical and oppressive. In the centre it had
once been paved, but never re-paved, and the cobbles were
thickly covered with a curly, low-growing weed which in the
afternoons, after the midday meal, gave out a sour, medicinal
sort of odour such as hovers around hospitals on hot days. For
a short distance, between the porter's quarters and the
carriage shed, the yard adjoined somebody else's garden.

It was here, behind the wood-pile, Zhenia made her way.
She propped up the ladder from underneath with a flat log,
wriggled it firm against the log-pile, which would give way, and
then seated herself, uncomfortably but very interestingly, on
the middle rung, like in a yard game. Then she got up and
climbed still higher and rested her book on the top rung, which
was broken, and thought now she really would read *The Demon*;
then, finding that the first place was the best to sit, she went
down again, forgetting her book on the top of the pile. She
forgot about it altogether because it was only now that she
suddenly noticed something on the other side of the garden
which she had never thought was there, and she gaped,
enchanted.

There were no bushes in this other garden, and the ancient
trees raised their lower branches up into the mass of leaves as

if up into a kind of night, leaving the garden below stripped naked, although it was always in a half-light, an airy, triumphant half-light, from which it never escaped. Those forked, thunder-blue limbs, grey blotched with lichen, permitted a full view of the deserted, unused little alley on to which that other garden opened. There was a yellow dogwood. The shrubbery was now dried up, shrivelled, the leaves fallen.

Thus translated by the gloomy garden into a new world, she saw the silent little alley beyond lit like events in a dream; that is, brilliant in detail but all very silent, as if there the sun had put on spectacles and was scrabbling about like a stupid old hen.

But what made Zhenia gape? Her discovery, more interesting to her than the people by whose help she made it.

There must be a shop there—outside the gate, in the street. And what a street! 'Lucky ones!' She was envious of the stranger girls. They were three in number.

They stood out black as the words 'fair captive' in the poem. Three even heads, back view, hair neat under round hats, were bent over something, as if the end one, half hidden by a tree trunk, was leaning on something else, asleep, and the others were asleep too, leaning on her. Their hats were blackish-grey-blue and the sunlight played on them in little spots like insects. They had black ribbons. Then the three strange girls turned their heads the other way. No doubt something in the street that way drew their attention. They spent a minute looking that other way, just as you look in summer when for a moment everything is dissolved by the light and lengthened so that you have to screw up your eyes and shield them with your hand— for that sort of minute they looked, then fell back to their former state of corporate drowsiness.

Zhenia would have gone home then, but when she felt for her book she could not recall at first where she had left it. She went back for it, and when she had climbed on to the wood-pile she saw that the three had got up and were going away. One after another they made their way to the gate. At their heels went a smallish man, walking with a limp. Under his arm he carried a huge book or atlas. So that was what they had been doing, peering over each other's shoulders. And she

27

had thought they were asleep. They crossed the garden and disappeared behind the outhouses. The sun was now nearly set. Getting her book Zhenia disturbed a log. The wood-pile came to life and the whole thing moved as if it were alive. A few logs rolled right down and ended up on the turf with a dull thump. It served as signal, like a watchman's rattle. Evening was now born, and with evening a host of sounds, tiny, haze-wrapped. The air began to pick out an old-time tune, a half whistle, from over the river.

The yard was empty. Prokhor had finished his work. He went out of the gateway, where, quite low down, right on the grass, like a sheet, was outspread the sad, reedy tinkle of a soldier's balalaika. Over it twirled and danced, broke away and fell, dissolved in the air, fell and dissolved, fell, and then before touching the earth soared high again, a thin, quiet swarm of midges. But the tinkle of the balalaika was even thinner, even quieter, swept lower towards the earth than the midges, and yet was clean of the dust, and better, more aery, than the swarm, sweeping high again, twinkling and breaking in the air, ever swooping, leisurely.

Zhenia went on her way indoors. 'Lame,' she said to herself—thinking of the stranger with the album—'lame, but a gentleman, no crutches.' She went the back way. The yard air held the persistent, pungent aroma of camomile. 'Lately Mummy's got a whole chemist's shop of little blue bottles with yellow labels.' Slowly she made her way up the steps. The iron railing was cold. Her feet shuffled and the steps creaked in answer. All of a sudden an extraordinary thought came into her head. She had just stepped two stairs at once, and now stood still on a third. What came into her head was that lately some intangible resemblance had appeared between her mother and the porter's wife. Something she simply could not make out. She stood still. It was something like—she thought of what— was it like what people meant when they said "We are all human . . ." or "We're all anointed with the same myrrh . . ." or "Fate doesn't distinguish blood . . ."? There was a little bottle on the stair and she pushed it away with her toe, and the bottle went down and fell onto the dusty matting without breaking. Anyway, something that was very, very, very common to all people. But if that was so, why was there not the same resemblance between herself and Axinia, or, say Axinia and Ouliasha? It seemed to Zhenia the more strange since it was difficult to find two people more unlike. Axinia had something earthy in her, like gardens, reminding you of potato clumps, or the greenery of wild pumpkins, whereas Mummy . . . The very thought of that comparison brought a scornful smile to Zhenia's lips.

Nevertheless it was Axinia and no one else who set the tone of that insistent comparison. She got the best of it too. The peasant wench gained nothing, but the *lady* did lose. For a brief space there was a very wild notion in Zhenia's mind: it occurred to her that some sort of elemental principle of the common people had entered her mother, and she imagined her mother even speaking with a vulgar accent and verbs all wrong; and could suddenly see the day coming when Mummy in her new silk gown, but beltless, like a barge, would be arms akimbo talking about "akeepin' t'doorpaost up!"

The passage reeked of medicine. Zhenia went straight to her father.

II

The house was redecorated, and luxury appeared. The Lüvers invested in a carriage and kept horses. The coachman's name was Davletsha.

At that time rubber tyres were the very latest. When they drove out everything turned round to stare at them: people, fences, church towers, barn-door cocks.

At the doctor's they were a long time opening the door to Mrs Lüvers, and when out of respect for her the carriage moved off slowly, she called after them "Don't go a long way, as far as the railway crossing and back; and take care on the hill," while, removing her from the doctor's doorstep, the pallid sun continued on its way down the street, reaching Davletsha's taut, florid, freckly neck, warming it up and making the little hairs stand on end.

29

They drove on to the bridge, and the chatter of its loose cross-timbers rang out all round them, crafty and full and harmonious (put together who knew when, for all time) cut short with all piety by the ravine beneath the bridge—by the never-forgettable sound of noon, of sleep.

Climbing the hill that overfed animal Vykormysh stumbled for foothold on the slippery, unyielding flint; he strained his withers, it was more than he could manage, and suddenly, in the scramble, reminiscent of a sprawling grasshopper, he became dazzlingly beautiful in the futility of his unnatural efforts, just as grasshoppers are aerial creatures by nature, and it seemed that any moment his patience would give out and with a furious flutter of wings he would soar away. And so he did. Up went his front legs and he was off over the vacant ground at a canter, with Davletsha trying to hold him in by tugging at the reins. A dog added its ragged, shaggy, uncomprehending bark, and the dust was like gunpowder. The road turned sharply to the left.

The black street ended blindly in the red wall of the railway goods depot. It was all alarm. The sun was slanting and wrapped round the crowd of strange figures in peasant blouses. The sun wrapped them in a stinging white light, which seemed to splash all over them as if somebody's jackboot had tipped over a bucket of thin mortar which was flooding over the ground. The street was all alarm. The horse was going at walking pace.

"Turn to the right," Zhenia ordered.

"We shan't be able to get through," Davletsha answered, and pointed with his huge whip to the red wall. "It's a blind alley."

"Then stop, I'll have a look."

"Those are our Chinese."

"So I see."

When Davletsha saw that the young lady was not going to discuss it with him, he gave a long-drawn-out sort of 'tprrrou', and the horse stopped as if frozen to the ground, all a-quiver. Then Davletsha set up a thin broken whistle, all little gushes and pauses, as fitted the moment.

The Chinese ran across the road with huge rye loaves in their hands. They were dressed in blue, like women in trousers.

30

Their bare heads ended in knots on the nape, and looked as if they were made of twisted-up handkerchiefs. Some of them stopped to watch, and Zhenia could look at those properly. Their faces were pale, earthen, grinning. They were sun-tanned and dirty, like brass oxidised by poverty. Davletsha took out his pouch and began to roll. And then from round the corner— from where the Chinese were making for—a number of women appeared. Also going for bread no doubt. Those in the road began guffawing, making their way up to them, with their hands behind their backs, as if pinioned there. Their wriggling movements were exaggerated by their being dressed, like acrobats, from head to heel in some kind of single garment. There was nothing really alarming in it; the women did not run away, but they too stopped, and laughed.

"Listen, Davletsha, what are you thinking about!"

The horse had dashed off—dashed off. He won't stand still, eh, won't stand still—and Davletsha tugged and shouted and lashed the horse with the reins.

"Steady there, you'll tip me out. What are you lashing him like that for?"

"I must."

And only when they had got out into the fields and the horse had quieted down—it had begun to dance madly—the crafty Tartar, having sped the young lady like an arrow from a shameful sight, took the reins in his right hand and tucked the pouch—which he had been holding all that time—back into the skirt of his coat.

They went back by another road. Mrs Lüvers had seen them, from the doctor's little window, no doubt. She came out on to the porch at the very instant that the bridge, which had already told them its story, started it all over again as the water-cart reached it.

III

With Liza Defendov, the girl who brought into class rowan berries gathered on the way to school, Zhenia made friends during one of the examinations. The daughter of the sacristan was

31

being re-examined in French, having failed first time. *Lüvers, Zhenia* was told to sit in the nearest empty place. Thus, sitting together at the same phrases, they made each other's acquaintance . . .

"*Est-ce Pierre qui a volé la pomme?*"

"*Oui, c'est Pierre qui vola, etc.* . . ."

And the acquaintanceship was not ended by the fact that Zhenia was taught at home. They began to meet each other. Their meetings, by mercy of her mother's overseeing eye, were one-sided. Liza was allowed to come to them, but so far Zhenia was not allowed to go to the Defendovs'.

The spasmodic nature of their meetings did not prevent Zhenia rapidly becoming very attached to her friend. She fell in love with her, that is to say, she became the suffering party in the relationship, the manometer, watchful and feverishly sensitive in the quivering of its needle. Every single mention Liza made of her class-mates, none of whom Zhenia knew, awakened in her sensations of desertion and gall. Her heart would sink. First intimations of jealousy. Without any reason for it, simply by force of her mistrustful conviction that Liza, outwardly so direct, but in her heart of hearts scornful of all in Zhenia that was Lüvers, was deceiving her, and behind her back, in school or at home, making mock of it—this Zhenia accepted as something which should be, implicit in the very nature of affection. Her feelings were as random in choice of object as could satisfy the imperative demands of that basic instinct which knows no self-love but solely the suffering and self-immolation that one sacrifices to any fetish when one first experiences it.

Neither Zhenia nor Liza had the least influence one on the other, but met and parted unchanged, one passionately feeling, the other feeling naught.

.   .   .   .   .

The father of the Akhmedianovs traded in iron. In the year between the birth of Nouretdin and Smagil he unexpectedly made money, and then Smagil was called Samoilo and the boys were to be brought up as Russians. Papa did not omit one single trait of the 'good old' devil-may-care Russian landowner mode of life, and did more than his bit in ten years' wild living in every direction. The children got on magnificently, that is, took after that fine example and inherited Papa's devil-may-care ways, loud, dashing, like a pair of flywheels set going and then left to the mercy of inertia. The most perfect fourth-form boys of all were the Akhmedianov brothers—a hurly-burly of crumbling chalk, shavings, gun-shot, thundering desks, indecent swear-words and snub-nosed, rosy-cheeked, frost-chapped impudence. Seriozha made friends with them in August. By the end of September the boy was quite shameless. Quite normal. Being a typical schoolboy and also a somebody besides, meant being in tow with the Akhmedianovs. And there was nothing Seriozha wanted more than to be a thorough-going schoolboy. Lüvers made no attempt to prevent his son's friendship. He noticed no change in him, or if he did notice anything, ascribed it to puberty. Besides, his head was full of other cares. It was about that time that he discovered he was ill, and that his illness was incurable.

IV

She was not sorry for him exactly, though nobody else had anything to say but how extraordinarily untimely it was and aggravating. Negarat was too spry even for Zhenia's parents and everything they felt about strangers was hazily communicated to the children too, as to spoiled pets. Zhenia was only grieved because things would not be as they used to be, and there would be no more of his laughter.

She happened to be at table the evening that he announced to her mother that he had to go to France, to Dijon, and do some kind of service. "Why, then, you must still be quite young," her mother said, and the flood-gates of her pity were immediately opened, while he sat there hanging his head. Conversation kept drying up. Her mother said: "The men are coming tomorrow to seal the windows," and she asked him if he wouldn't like them shut now. He said no, the evening was warm, and in his country the windows weren't sealed up at all, even in mid-winter. Shortly after that her father turned up, and he too poured forth his regrets at the news. But before he began his wailing he did raise his eyebrows and ask in surprise:

"Dijon? But surely you are a Belgian, aren't you?"

"I am, but I am a French subject." And Negarat then told the story of his 'old folks' migration, so interestingly, as if he were not their son, with as much warmth indeed as if talking about some strangers he had read about in a book.

"Excuse me if I interrupt you a moment," her mother said. "Zhenia, my pet, all the same, do shut that window, there's a dear."

Then, to her father:

"Vika, the men are coming tomorrow to do them up. Do please go on. Whatever you say, that uncle of yours was a real old scoundrel. Do you mean to say he really did *swear* to it?"

"He did."

And he returned to his interrupted story. And when at last he reached the point, which was the paper he had received the preceding day by post from the Consulate, he guessed that the young lady could not make head or tail of it all, but was trying to, so he began explaining, but in such a way as not to show what he was doing in order not to touch her on the quick, explaining exactly what military service meant.

"Yes, yes, I understand. Yes, I understand, I do really," she assured him with mechanical gratitude.

"Why on earth go so far? Be a soldier here, that is to say," she corrected herself, "study where the others do"—and vividly saw in her imagination the green meadows spread out below the priory hill.

"Yes, yes, I understand. Yes I do," the girl went on, and Mr and Mrs Lüvers, sitting there out of it, and thinking that this Belgian was overloading the child's head with unnecessary detail, every now and then put in their sleepy simplifications. And suddenly came the minute when she felt sorry for all who had even long ago, or even quite recently, been Negarats in any distant place, and then bidding farewell all round, had set out on that unwanted, unsought-for journey, to be soldiers in this alien city of Ekaterinburg. This man made it all so clear to her. Nobody hitherto had done this. A rush of heartlessness, a shattering rush of vividness, was stripped from her white-tent picture of regiments, tarnished now and turned into a collection of individual men in soldier's clothes, who became pitiable the very moment that this reasonability suddenly introduced into them brought them to life and elevated them, so that they ceased to be a colourful picture, but become merely near and dear ones.

Good-byes.

"I shall leave part of my books with Tzvetkov. That's the friend I have told you so much about. Please make use of them as hitherto, *Madame*. Your son knows where I live, he is often at my landlord's house, and I'm handing over my room to Tzvetkov. I shall tell him about the books."

"Tell him to come in and see us. Tzvetkov, you say his name is?"

"That's right, Tzvetkov."

"Tell him to come to see us. We shall make him welcome. When I was younger I knew . . ." and she shot a look at her husband, who was standing right against Negarat, his hands tucked under his close-fitting jacket, waiting for a convenient gap in this exchange of politenesses, so he might make a final arrangement with the Belgian about the next day.

"Yes, tell him he's to come to see us. Only not just now. I'll send him an invitation. Yes, take it, it's yours. I could not finish it. It made me cry so. The doctor advised me to stop reading it altogether. To avoid excitement." And once again she gave her husband a look. He lowered his face and with creaking collar, breathing heavily, began to peer down, very anxious to see if both his boots were on and then if both were well cleaned.

"So there we are. Well, well. Don't forget your stick. We shall see each other again, I trust."

"Why, of course, I don't leave till Friday. What day is it today?" He showed that sudden fright of people who are leaving.

35

"Wednesday. It is Wednesday, isn't it, Vika? Vika, it is Wednesday, isn't it?" And then her father at last got his edge in. "Wednesday . . . *Ecoutez, demain . . .*" and walked out to the landing with Negarat.

V

They strode on, talking, and from time to time she had to give a hop, skip and a run to keep up with Seriozha and get back in step with him. They were walking very fast, and her raincoat slipped down on her shoulders, because to help herself along she was working her arms, but she was also keeping her hands in her pockets. It was cold and the thin ice crackled merrily under her snow-shoes. They were on an errand for their mother—to buy a present for the man who was to go, and they were talking.

"So they were taking him to the station, were they?"

"Mhm!"

"But why was he sitting in straw?"

"How do you mean?"

"In the wagon. All in straw. Legs covered. People don't sit like that."

"I've already told you. Because he was a criminal."

"So they are taking him to hard labour?"

"No. To Perm. There's no prison department here. Watch where you tread."

They had to cross the street past the tinsmith's. All the summer the shop door had been wide open and Zhenia had grown accustomed to seeing the crossing dominated by that blast of general and friendly liveliness which the fierce gaping mouth of the workshop gave forth. All July, August and September, carts stopped outside it, blocking the crossing; peasants waited about, mainly Tatars; a confusion of buckets and guttering, broken and rusty. There more than anywhere the dense sun sank strangely into the dusk at the hour when over the next-door fence their neighbours cut the throats of young fowls; and as it sank, transformed the crowd to an encampment and painted the Tatars like Gypsies. Front axle-trees, freed from the hooded wagons, their shafts smooth-worn by harness, cut hollows in the velvet dust.

The cauldrons and the scrap-iron were still there, left where they had fallen; only now patined with frost; but the doors were tightly closed, as if it was a holiday on account of the cold, and the crossing was a desert. Out of a round ventilation hole came Zhenia's familiar musty scent of burning metal, hissing noisily, acrid to her nostrils, only then settling on to her palate, prickly, like cheap lemonade.

"Is there a prison department in Perm then?"

"Yes. A Prison Board. I think we'd better go this way. It's nearer. There is one at Perm, because Perm's a government town, and Ekaterinburg is only a provincial centre. It's too small."

The path along past the villas was paved with red brick and bordered with shrubs. There were traces of the hazy and enfeebled sun on it. Seriozha walked as loudly as he could.

"If you tickle this berberis with a pin in the spring when it's flowering, it flutters all its leaves, just as if it were alive."

"I know."

"And you're afraid of being tickled aren't you?"

"Yes."

"That means you're highly-strung; the Akhmedianovs say that if anyone is afraid of being tickled . . ."

And on they went—Zhenia trotting, Seriozha striding with astounding strides, and her raincoat slipping down on her shoulders. They caught sight of Dikikh just as the wicket-gate, swinging on its post like a turnstile, held them up. They caught sight of him from a good distance. He had just come out of the very shop they were now half a block from. Dikikh was not alone; he was followed by a man of medium height who tried to hide a slight limp as he walked. Zhenia could not help thinking she had seen that man somewhere before. They passed without greeting each other. The others cut across the street, and Dikikh did not notice the children. He had on high goloshes, and kept lifting up his arms with his fingers spread wide. He *simply did not agree* and all ten fingers had to help prove that the other man . . . (But where was it she had seen that other man? A long time ago. But where? It must have been in Perm, *when she was a child*.)

"Wait a moment!" How annoying. Seriozha knelt down. "Just a second."

"Caught on a nail?"

"Of course. Idiots, don't even know how to knock a nail in properly!"

"All right?"

"Oh, do wait a moment. I can't find it. I know that fellow with the limp. Ah, there it is. Thank heaven."

"Torn it?"

"No, fortunately. That's an old hole in the lining. I didn't do that. Well, let's get on. Half a moment, just clean my knee. All right, come on."

"I know who it is. He lives in the Akhmedianovs' house. Where Negarat used to live. Do you remember I told you how people collect there and drink all night; you can see the light in their windows. Remember? Remember when I spent the night there? Samoilo's birthday. Well, one of those. Remember?"

Yes, she remembered. She saw she had been mistaken, as, if Seriozha was right, she could not have seen the lame man in Perm, that was only an illusion. But still it seemed so to her, and being taciturn when she had ideas like that, turning over everything of Perm she could recall, she followed her brother, making this or that movement, holding on to this or that, stepping over this or that, and then looked round her and found she was in the half-light of counters and light cardboard boxes and shelves and over-anxious good-afternoons and attention—and . . . Seriozha was speaking.

The book they wanted the bookseller (who sold all sorts of tobacco) had not got, but he reassured them and averred that the Turgeniev was definitely coming, in fact had been sent from Moscow, was on the way, and that it was only a minute or so ago that he had been talking about it to Mr Tzvetkov himself, that is to say, to their schoolmaster. His slippery tongue and the illusion he was under tickled the two children mightily and they said *good afternoon* and went out empty-handed.

Once outside, Zhenia turned to her brother.

"Seriozha, I always forget to ask you; do you know the street we can see from our wood-pile?"

"No. Never been there."

"That's a lie. I've seen you myself."

"From the wood-pile? You . . ."

"Well, no, not from the wood-pile, but in that street, on the other side of Cherep-Savvich's garden."

"Oh, that's what you're thinking of. You're right. You can see it as you go by. The other side of the garden in the background. Some sheds and a wood-pile. I say, so that's *our* courtyard? That yard? Ours? Why, I'd never realized that! And how often I've been by there and thought how fine it would be to get up there once, on that wood, and then on the roof—I've seen a ladder up there. So that's our own yard?"

"Seriozha, will you show me the way there?"

"What, again? But it's our yard. What's there to show? You know——"

"Seriozha, you never understand me. I'm talking about the street, and you're talking about the yard. Show me the way to that street. Show me how to get there. You will, Seriozha, won't you?"

"But still I don't understand. Why, we've just been down it—and we'll be there again in a minute."

"You don't say so!"

"But of course. And the coppersmith? At the corner."

"So then that dusty street . . ."

"Why, of course, the one you keep asking me about! The Cherep-Savviches are at the end, on the right. Oh, don't hang behind, we mustn't be late for dinner. There's crayfish today."

They began to talk of something else. The Akhmedianovs had promised to teach him to tin samovars. And as for her question about what tin was, tin was a kind of mountain rock, otherwise ore, like lead, only dull. It was used for lining cans and mending pots, and the Akhmedianovs knew how to do all that.

Then they had to run across the street or a train of wagons would have kept them back. That made them both forget— she her request about that little-used alley, and Seriozha about his promise to show it her. They passed the door of the shop, where Zhenia drew in a sharp breath of that warm greasy smoke which you get when you clean brass door-handles and candle-sticks, and then remembered where she had once seen that stranger, him and the three strange girls, and what they were doing. The next instant she realized that the Mr Tzvetkov the bookseller had spoken about was that very same man with the limp.

VI

Negarat left by an evening train. Her father went to see him off. He did not get back from the station till late at night, and his appearance caused a tremendous disturbance in the porter's lodge, which did not subside for a long time. People went out with lanterns and they were shouting for somebody. It was pouring with rain and somebody's geese were loose and making a din.

Day rose gloomy and shaky. The wet grey street danced as if rubber, and there was a nasty drizzle fluttering down and spattering mud about. Wagon wheels sloshed and squelched as they passed. People in goloshes.

Zhenia was on her way home. There were still echoes of the night's disturbance about in the yard; she was not able to have the carriage. She had said she was going to the shop for some hemp seed, and ran round to see her friend; but when half-way there she felt sure she would never find her way alone from the shop to the Defendovs' house, so she turned back. Then she remembered that it was too early anyway— Liza would be at school. She was now thoroughly soaked and was shivering with cold. The sky was clearing under the stiff wind, but it was still raining. There was a cold white hard light which ripped down the street and clung to the wet paving-stones in sheets. The gloomy clouds were speeding away out of the town; at the end of the square beyond the three-armed street lamp they grew panicky and piled one on top of the other.

To move like that he must have been either a very slovenly person or unprincipled. The furniture of a rather poor study was not packed on the dray, but simply stood on it just as it had stood in the room, and the castors of the arm-chairs peeping out from under the white dust-covers rolled to and fro every time the wagon tipped one way or the other. The covers were snowy white in spite of being soaked through. They were so striking that you only needed to glance at them, for the cobbles, gnawed bare by the rains, for the shivering cold puddles against the fence, for the birds flying from the stables, for the trees flying after them, for the patches of lead, and even that *ficus* in the tub which swayed and bowed clumsily to all things flying by, to turn the same colour.

That was a crazy load. It made everybody look at it. There was a peasant striding beside it: the platform tipped right over as it moved slowly forward, the wheels plunging into potholes. And over all this croaking tattered thing hung a wet leaden-coloured word—*town*, which in her mind gave rise to a host of ideas as transient as that chill October light which winged past her and fluttered to the wet street.

"He'll catch cold; he'll only ruin his things," she said to herself, of the unknown owner. And she imagined the man— *an abstract sort of man, like a roller, step by step staggering about putting his bits of property in their respective places.* She had a vivid picture of how he got hold of things and how he moved, and particularly how he took a duster and poked about round the tub and wiped the wetted leaves of his *ficus*. After which followed sneezes, a cold, a temperature. That without fail. Zhenia could see that most vividly too. Most vividly. The wagon rumbled away up towards Isseti. Zhenia had to turn left.

.   .   .   .   .

It must have been somebody's heavy footsteps outside. The tea in the glass on the little table by her bed rose and sank

41

again. The piece of lemon in the tea rose and sank again. The rays of sunlight on the wallpaper swayed to and fro, like pillars, like the glass tubes with coloured syrup in the shops behind the curtains with Turks smoking. Behind the curtains with Turkains, the Turtains with Curcains, the Curcains with . . . curtains . . . smoking. . . .

It must have been somebody's heavy footsteps. The little patient fell asleep again.

Zhenia had gone down the day after Negarat left, the very day when coming home from her walk she learned that Axinia had had a baby in the night: the day she had seen the wagon of the man who was moving, and concluded that rheumatism had its eyes on him. Her fever lasted a fortnight; painful red pepper all over her, burning her, making her sweat, gumming up her eyes and lips. The steaminess was troublesome, and her sense of taste was mixed up with a horrid feeling of fatness. As if a summer wasp had filled her with a flame and it was blowing her up. As if, like a little grey hair, the wasp's fine sting was still in her and she wanted to pull it out, over and over again, all ways out. Out of her purple temples, out of her shoulder, gasping in the fire under her nightdress, everywhere. Now she was getting better again. She felt weak all over.

For example, this sense of weakness, it risked everything and showed itself in a strange geometry *all of its own*, which made her a little dizzy and sick at times.

For example, beginning from an episode on the counterpane, the sense of weakness set to piling on it layer on layer of ever-greater spaces, that soon became unbelievably big in that striving of the twilight to assume the shape of a public square which was the very basis of that vagary of space. Or else, starting out from a pattern of the wallpaper, it would drive broadnesses row after row up towards her, gliding as if greased, one replacing the other, and also, like all those sensations, wearing you down by their steady and regular growth in sheer size. Or else it tortured her ill body with depths which went endlessly lower and lower, revealing their bottomlessness from the very outset, from the very first thing in the parquet, then lowered her bed towards the bottom, gently, gently, and her with the bed. Then her head would be in the position of a lump of sugar cast on to the high tide of terrible, empty, unseasoned chaos, and be dissolved in it, melting away in transparent whorls.

This was caused by heightened sensitivity of the oral labyrinths.

It was somebody's heavy footsteps. The lemon sank and then rose again. Also the sun on the wallpaper rose and sank constantly. At last she woke up. Her mother came in and congratulated her on being better at last, and seemed to her to be able to read her thoughts. As she was coming to she had heard something about it. That was—the congratulations of her own arms and legs and elbows and knees, congratulations from them as she stretched her body. It was their congratulations indeed that wakened her. And now Mummy too. What a strange coincidence!

The whole household was now in and out, sitting on her bed a few moments and then off again. She put question after question, and they answered. There were things which had changed during her illness; others were unchanged. Those unchanged she did not bother about, but she could not let the others alone. Apparently Mummy herself was unchanged, and Daddy was quite obviously exactly the same. But these had changed: she herself, Seriozha, the distribution of light in the room, the quietness of everybody else, and still other things, ever so many things. Had the winter snow come yet? No. There had been snow, then a thaw, then a bit of frost, nobody knew what they were coming to, everything was bare, no snow at all. She scarcely noticed whom she questioned, or about what. The answers got all tangled. Those who were well came and went. Liza came. They would not let her in at first. Then they remembered that you cannot catch measles twice, and let her in. Dikikh came. She scarcely noticed who gave her what answer. When they all went to dinner, and she was alone with Ouliasha, she remembered how they had all laughed in the kitchen at a silly question of hers. She then took care not to do the same again. She had put an intelligent, business-like question—like a grown-up. She had asked if Axinia was in the

43

family way again. That made the girl drop a spoon as she was clearing away, and turn to one side. "Oh, well I never. . . . Now do let her get her breath. . . . Zhenia, my pet, she can't have them all at one go." And she ran out and shut the door firmly. And then Zhenia had heard the whole kitchen roar with laughter, as if the swirl of shrill chatter, the charwoman and Galim being the butts, and the din rising steadily till it seemed they had passed from teasing to fighting, when someone came and closed the door which they had forgotten.

So that question she must not ask. That would be sillier still.

VII

What, surely not thawing again? So today again they would go out in the carriage, and still could not put it on the runners? Zhenia would spend hours standing at the little window, till her nose was cold and her hands frozen. Dikikh had just gone. He was displeased with her now. But she would like to see anyone learn her lessons there in the house, with the cocks crowing about the yards all round, and the sky a-buzz, and when that died down, then the cocks again. Clouds dirty and tattery, like a moth-eaten sleigh-rug. The day thrust its snout against the window-pane like a calf in its steamy stall. Why was it not spring? But after dinner the air gripped everything in a hoop of grey cold, the sky wrinkled and shrank, and you could hear the clouds' wheezy breathing. As if impatient for the winter dusk, impatient for the north, the flitting hours rent the last leaves from the trees, stripped the lawns bare, pierced through crevices and tore at people's bodies. The nozzles of the northern Mother Earth began to show dark beyond the house-tops: they were pointing directly at their yard, loaded with a huge November. But it was still only October.

But it was still only October; there had not been a winter like this in living memory. People were saying the autumn-sown wheat had perished and there was famine to be feared. As if someone had taken a sceptre and waved it and passed it over chimneys and roofs and the boxes for the starlings, next

Spring, saying—smoke here, snow here, hoarfrost here. But there was neither snow nor frost. The desert, wilted twilight, pined for them. They strained their eyes, and the earth ached from early lighting in the streets and fires in the houses, just as one's head aches from long expectation and the misery of strained eyes. Everything was tense, expectant; winter wood was stocked in the kitchens, the clouds had been bursting with snow for a fortnight, the air was heavy with darkness. When would that magician who managed it all, whom one's eye could see, when would he swirl his magic circles and pronounce his curse and summon winter, the spirit of which was surely waiting at the door?

Yet how slack they had been, neglecting it so. It's true they never paid much attention to the calendar in the classroom. She tore the pages off her own. But all the same! August the twenty-ninth! Cunning, as Seriozha would have said. A Red-letter Day. *The Beheading of John the Baptist.* It came off its nail easily. Having nothing better to do she set about tearing the old leaves off. A monotonous job, so that after a while she simply forgot what her fingers were doing, though from time to time she would mutter: "Thirtieth—so now for the thirty-first."

"It's three days since she set foot out of doors!" Those words, heard in the corridor, wrenched her back from her daydream, and she saw how far she had got. Past *The Presentation of the Virgin* even. Her mother touched her hand.

"Zhenia, what is the meaning of this . . ."

The rest of her mother's words might not have been spoken. As if wakening from a dream Zhenia asked her mother to say *The Beheading of John the Baptist.* Her mother said it, thoroughly puzzled. She did not pronounce it at all like Axinia.

The very next minute Zhenia was astounded at her own self. What on earth was that? Whoever suggested that to her? Wherever had that come from? Had she, Zhenia, really asked her mother that? Or was it possible she had really thought her mother . . . ? How fantastic, how unreal! Whose invention now was that . . . ?

All this time her mother stood looking at her, unable to

45

believe her ears, staring at her wide-open eyes. This astonishing
sally really puzzled her. The question looked like mockery;
but her little daughter's eyes were swimming with tears.

·   ·   ·   ·   ·

Those hazy presentiments of hers came true. When out for
a drive she heard the air grow softer, saw the clouds melt
inwards, heard the click of hoofs muffle. The street lamps were
still not lit when little grey tufts of dry down began to wander
through the air. But they had not even reached the bridge
when those few scattered flakes gave place to a solid wall of
snow swooping down on them. Davletsha jumped down and
raised the leather hood. Then Zhenia and Seriozha found it
dark and tight inside. Zhenia wanted to be furious like the
furious storm outside. They noticed that Davletsha was driving
them home simply because they again heard the bridge under
Vykormish's hoofs. The streets were unrecognizable; there
were no streets left. Night had descended in an instant: the
town lost its head and was one solid stir of countless thousands
of pale lips. Seriozha leant out and, supporting himself with
his knee, told Davletsha to drive to the workshop row. Zhenia
caught her breath in ecstasy, beheld all the delights and
charms of winter in the way Seriozha's words rang out in the
air. Davletsha shouted back that they would have to go
straight home, not to tire the horse too much, as the master and
mistress were going to the theatre, and he would have to put
the carriage on runners, too. Zhenia then remembered that
Mummy and Daddy would be out, and she would be alone. She
made up her mind at once to make herself ever so comfy by
the lamp and have a good long read at the volume of *The
Fables of Pussy-cat* which were 'only for grown-ups'. She would
have to get it out of Mummy's bedroom. And some chocolate.
And then read, munching at chocolate, and listen to the sound
of the streets being swept outside.

Oh, but it was coming down properly now, and no mistaking
it. The skies shuddered and from them out came foundering
whole white empires and continents without end. And they

were both mysterious and frightful. It was clear that those falling worlds (who knew whence) had never heard either of life or of this world, or the earth, and being midnight things and blind they smothered it, because they neither saw it nor knew about it.

They were ravishingly frightful, those empires; absolutely satanically rapturous. Zhenia caught her breath as she gazed on them. And the air staggered to and fro, grasping at that falling universe, and far, far away, in pain, oh, in what pain, the countryside howled as if seared by whips. Everything was confusion. Night rushed at them, infuriated by that single grey hair, low fallen, which cut into it and blinded it. Everything was scattered far and wide, shrieking, no matter where. And hailing cry and wailing answer alike were lost, never met, died, over many roofs, swept away by the blizzard. Blinding.

They stamped and stamped in the hall, and shook the snow off their fluffy short white fur coats. And what pools of water running from the goloshes on to the check linoleum! The table was covered with egg-shells, the pepper-pot had been taken out of the cruet and not put back, there was a lot of pepper spilt on the table-cloth, and on the yolk which had run out and in the tin with the unfinished 'seredines'—Wednesday fish!* Father and mother had already had their supper, but were still sitting in the dining-room, and trying to hurry the children, who dawdled. They did not scold them, because they had supped long before their time, as they were going to the theatre. Mummy could not make up her mind now whether to go or not, and was ever so sad. When she saw her mother, Zhenia too remembered that really she ought not to be the least happy herself—oh, at last she got that rotten fastener undone—rather, she ought to be sad, and when she came into the dining-room she asked what had been done with the walnut cake. Then her father looked at her mother and said nobody was forcing them, and so they might as well stay at home.

"No, why," mummy said, "after all I ought to have some amusement, the doctor gave permission."

* In Russian Wednesday is *sereda*, or "middle" (sc. of the week).

"Well, make up your mind."

"But where is that cake?" Zhenia asked again. For answer she got the information that the cake would not run away, that there were other things to eat before she got to the cake, that nobody began supper with cake, the cake was in the cupboard—just as if she had never been in the house before, had just arrived, and did not know where things were kept. Her father said all this, and then turned to her mother again and said:

"Make up your mind."

"It's made up, we'll go."

And, with a sad smile at Zhenia, her mother went to dress. While Seriozha, tapping his egg with the egg-spoon and taking care not to miss, announced to his father in business-like fashion, as if very busy, that the weather had changed—there was a blizzard, he ought to bear that in mind—and burst out laughing. Now that his nose had thawed out it was not behaving as it should, and he screwed up his face, then got his handkerchief out of the pocket of his tight uniform breeches and blew it just as his father had taught him, 'so as not to damage the ear-drums', then got busy with the egg-spoon again, and, looking his father straight in the face, his own cheeks ruddy from the drive and freshly washed, said:

"Just as we were going out we saw Negarat's friend. You know."

"Evans?" his father asked, absent-mindedly.

"We don't know that man," Zhenia cried hotly.

"Vika!" came from the bedroom.

Their father got up and answered the call. In the doorway Zhenia came on Ouliasha, bringing her a lighted lamp. Soon the door next to hers banged to. That was Seriozha, gone to his room. He was magnificent today, his sister loved the Akhmedianovs' friend to be a real boy, and she loved to be able to speak of his wearing the high-school uniform.

Doors opening and shutting. Stamping about in snow-boots. At last *they* had gone, the master and mistress. The letter informed Ouliasha that she 'up to now had not been so nice about asking and you might as well say what you want now just the same', and when the 'dear sister', loaded with presents and assurances had gone through the whole family saying who was to have what, Ouliasha, who now turned out to be a dignified 'Ouliava', said "Thank you" to her young mistress, turned the lamp down and left the room, taking with her the letter, the ink-well and a greasy piece of octavo paper that was left.

Then Zhenia applied herself again to her homework. She did not put the figures in brackets. She went on dividing away, copying out figure after figure. There seemed to be no end to it. Endless recurring decimals. 'What if measles kept recurring,' she thought suddenly: 'Dikikh today said something about infinity.' She no longer knew what she was doing. She felt that that afternoon something of the same sort had happened to her, and she had also wanted to sleep or cry, but when it was and what was really the matter she could not make out—because she had not the strength to think of anything. The noise outside had subsided. The blizzard was gradually dying down. Decimal fractions were quite new to her. There was no room on the right, and she decided to start over again, write smaller, and check every figure. Outside it was deathly silent now. She was afraid of forgetting what she had borrowed and not carrying the right figure over.

'The window won't run away,' she said to herself, continuing to pour three's and seven's into bottomless space, 'and I shall hear them in good time; it's quiet everywhere; they won't come up at once; they'll have their furs on, and Mother pregnant; but the point is, 3737 goes on repeating, I can either go on copying it out or . . .' And suddenly recalled that that was just what Dikikh had been saying only an hour or so ago—that she *need not divide out, but simply discard them.* She rose and went to the window.

It was now clear outside. Only rare flakes swam out of the darkness into the light of the street lamp, floated up, sailed round it and vanished again. In their place new ones. The street glistened with the dignified snow-white carpet spread over it. It was white, bright and sweet like candied cakes in fairy stories. Zhenia stood some time at the window gazing at those circles and figures which the Andersenian silvery snowflakes performed. And then she went to Mummy's room for the *Cat* book. She went without a light. She could see without one. The stable roof filled the room with a ceaseless sparkle. The beds froze under the sigh of that huge roof and glittered. Here in disorder lay discarded smoky silk. Diminutive little bodices gave out an oppressive and stuffy odour of armpits and calico. There was the scent of violets and the cupboard was bluish dark, like the night outside, and like that dry warm darkness in which those freezing-cold glitterings moved. One of the knobs of the bed gleamed, a lonely bead. The other was extinguished by a slip thrown over it. Zhenia half closed her eyes, and the bead separated from the floor and moved towards the wardrobe. Then she remembered what she had come in for. Book in hand she went to one of the bedroom windows. It was a starry night. Winter had arrived in Ekaterinburg. She looked out into the yard and her thoughts turned to Pushkin. She made up her mind to ask her tutor to give her an essay to do on Onegin.

Seriozha wanted to talk. He said:

"You been putting scent on yourself? Give me some."

He had been very sweet all day. He was very red in the face. And she could not help thinking that perhaps there never would be such an evening again. She wanted to be alone.

She went back to her own room and set about reading the cat stories. She read one and began another, holding her breath. She was so absorbed in it she did not hear her brother going to bed in the next room. An extraordinary sort of game now began of its own accord to play over her face. She was not aware of it. At one moment her features swam out of shape and turned fish-face; her lower lip dangled and her lifeless pupils, fixed by fear to the page, refused to rise, afraid of finding *it* behind the tall-boy. Then she suddenly began nodding to the printed letters, as if in sympathy with them, as if approving them, just as people approve something somebody has done and are pleased at the turn events have taken. She dawdled over reading the descriptions of lakes and rushed headlong ahead into the dense mass of nocturnal scenes with a fragment of guttering Bengal fire on which their illumination depended. In one place a character was lost and shouted at intervals and then listened carefully for a reply, but heard only his own echo. So intent was she then that her throat began to tickle and caused a fit of coughing. The un-Russian name of Myrrha brought her back to reality. She put the book on one side and lost herself in thought. 'So that's what winter is like in Asia. I wonder what those Chinese are doing now, on so dark a night?' Her eyes fell on the clock. 'How creepy it must be to be with Chinese in this darkness.' Zhenia looked at the clock again, and was horrified. Any moment her parents might come home. It was well on the way to twelve o'clock. She unlaced her boots and then remembered she had to put the book back in its place.

.   .   .   .   .

Zhenia started from her sleep. She sat up in bed, eyes starting out of her head. This was no burglar. There were a number of people and they were running about and talking loudly, as if it were daytime. Suddenly somebody shrieked out as if their throat had been cut, and something was dragged along, chairs were knocked over. It was a woman shrieking. Gradually Zhenia recognized them all; all but the woman. An extraordinary chasing-about began, doors banging. When the farthest door banged it seemed somebody was trying to stop the woman shrieking by putting a hand on her mouth. But she got free and scaled the whole flat with a burning knife-like cry. Zhenia's hair stood on end, because the woman was her mother; and *Zhenia guessed*. There was Ouliasha lamenting and then after catching her father's voice once Zhenia did not get it again. Then Seriozha was being pushed in somewhere, and bellowing "You daren't lock me in".

"There are no strangers"—and just as she was, barefoot in her little nightie, Zhenia rushed out into the passage. Her father nearly fell over her. He had not taken his overcoat off. As he ran past he shouted something to Ouliasha.

"Papa!"

She saw him come running back with the marble basin from the bathroom.

"Papa!"

"Where's Lipa?" she heard him shout as he ran, beside himself.

Splashing water on to the floor, he disappeared inside, and when a second later he reappeared, coatless and in shirtsleeves, Zhenia found herself wrapped in Ouliasha's arms, but did not catch what was being said in that desperate, deep, exhausted whisper.

"What's the matter with Mummy?"

By way of answer Ouliasha kept on saying:

"You mustn't Zhenia, pet, you mustn't, darling, go to sleep, wrap yourself up in bed, lie on your little side. Ah, O, Lord God Almighty!"

You mustn't, you mustn't, she kept on saying, wrapping her away from it, as if she were a baby, and taking her away; *you mustn't, you mustn't,* but what she *mustn't* was never said, only Ouliasha's face was wet and her hair all tangled. A key turned on her, three doors away.

Zhenia lit a match to see if it would soon be daylight. It was only a little after twelve. That surprised her very much. Was it possible she had not been asleep even one hour? Meanwhile the noise in the other part of the flat did not die down. Howls broke out, exploding, riddling the house. Then for a short instant there succeeded an immense silence, eternity. This silence swallowed up hasty steps and quick, cautious speech. Then there was a ring of the door-bell. Then another. Then so much talk and disputing and ordering about that it seemed the flat would be burned away by all those voices, like tables under a thousand extinguished candelabra.

Zhenia fell asleep. Crying. Dreamed there were visitors. Kept counting them and getting them wrong. Every time she got one too many. And every time she made the same mistake she felt the same horror that she had felt when she realized it was none other than her mother.

. . . . .

How could anybody help being glad to see such a bright clear morning. Seriozha at once thought of out-door games, snowballing, fights with the yard kids. They had their morning tea in the class-room. They were told the floor polishers were in the dining-room. Their father came in. It was obvious at once that he did not know anything about the floor polishers. He did not know a single thing about them. He told them the real true cause of this move. Their mother had been taken ill. She needed quiet. Untrammelled and buoyant in their cawing, rooks flew by over the white film of street. A sleigh swooped past, pushing a miserable little horse in front of it. The horse was not used to the new thing behind it and missed its step.

"You're going to stay with the Defendovs, I've made all the arrangements. And you . . ."

"Why?" Zhenia interrupted him.

But Seriozha had guessed why and before his father could speak, said:

"Because of the infection of course."

But the street outside would not let him go on and he ran to the window as if someone had beckoned him. A Tatar, out in new rig, was a magnificent sight, like a cock pheasant. Lambskin high cap on his head. And his sheepskin overcoat, wool inside, blazed brighter than morocco leather. He walked with a roll, no doubt because that raspberry-coloured fish-boning on his white winter boots was completely oblivious of the construction of human joints; those arabesques sprawled all over the place, little caring whether they were on boots or tea-cups or roof guttering. But the most noticeable thing was—just at that moment the groans feebly coming from the bedroom grew louder, and Father went out into the passage, and told them they were not to follow him—the most noticeable thing was the track he made with them, a narrow clear-cut little ribbon across the smooth expanse. So clean and neat, squashed to ice, they made the snow look even whiter and more satin-like.

"Here's a note, which you'll give to Mr Defendov. To nobody else, understand? Well, come along, get your clothes on. Ouliasha'll be here with them in a moment. You'll go out by the back door. And the Akhmedianovs are expecting you."

53

"Ho, really expecting me, are they!" Seriozha was saucy.
"Yes. Dress in the kitchen."

Father seemed very distracted, as he led them slowly into
the kitchen, where there was a heap of coats and caps and
mittens on a stool ready for them. A gust of winter air swirled
up the shaft of the stairs. The sleighs swished past outside
with a scroop and a sigh. The children were all in a hurry and
they could not find their sleeve-holes. Their things smelt of
chests and sleepy furs.

"What are you doing!"

"Don't stand it on the edge, it'll fall off. Well, how now?"

"Still groaning."

The kitchen-maid gathered her apron in her hands and
stooped and grabbed some wood: as she opened the stove door
to stuff it in, the fierce flame gasped. "Not my doing" she
muttered indignantly, as she went back to her own world. In
a battered black old pail was a mess of broken glass and yellow
prescriptions. The towels were soaked with shaggy, lumpy
blood. They blazed. One felt one wanted to stamp them out,
like smouldering tinder. The stove was covered with saucepans
of water heating. All about the kitchen were white cups and
mortars, of shapes they had never seen, like at the chemist's.
In the hall little Galim was cracking ice. Seriozha wanted to
know if there was still much of last year's ice left.

"There'll soon be fresh ice," he said. "Give me some. What
are you wasting it for?"

"Whatcher mean, wastin' it? I gotta break it up for
t'bottles."

"Now then there, are you ready?"

No. Zhenia had run back into the house again. Seriozha
went out on to the landing and while he waited for her, he
drummed on the iron railing with a piece of firewood.

VIII

The Defendov household were just about to begin supper.
Grandmother Defendov crossed herself and flopped heavily

into her arm-chair. The lamp burned badly and was smoking; first they turned it too high, then too low, time and again. Defendov's bony hand was always reaching out to the screw, and when he slowly took his hand away from the lamp and sat back again his hand shook, not like an old man's, but with a tiny quivering, as if he was lifting a wineglass filled brimful. It was the tips of his fingers quivered, from the nail down.

He spoke in an even voice with precise enunciation, just as if his talking did not consist of sounds, but was built up out of separate letters, and he pronounced everything, even the letters which didn't sound.

The bulbous globe of the lamp glowed fierce between the whiskers provided by the geranium and the heliotrope. Cockroaches huddled close to the warmth and the hands of the clock reached cautiously over towards it. And time crept by in the way it does in winter. This was where it ripened to a head. Outside it was set rigid, foul-smelling. Under the window it was all fuss, poking about to one side and the other, doubling and trebling in little tongues of light.

Mrs Defendov put the roast on the table. Clouds of steam rose; seasoned with onion. Defendov made a little speech full of "I heartily recommend," and Liza's tongue never stopped once, but Zhenia heard neither of them. She had wanted to cry all day, because of yesterday, and now the longing grew desperate. Cry in that blouse too, made exactly as Mummy ordered.

Defendov guessed what was the matter, and did his best to take her mind off it, which meant that one moment he would try talking to her as if she were a babe in arms, and the next, fly off to the other extreme. His jocular questions frightened her and made her feel awkward. He fumbled and fingered the soul of this little friend of his daughter, just as if he was asking her heart how old it was. As soon as he was *unquestionably* certain of any little trait, he harped on it to try and make her forget her own home, but merely succeeded in reminding her that she was among strangers.

At last she could stand it no longer. She suddenly stood up and, shy as any child might well be, muttered:

"Thank you. I've really had enough. Can I go and look at pictures?"

And then, blushing crimson when she saw the general astonishment on all faces, nodded towards the middle room and said:

"Walter Scott. May I?"

"Of course, dearie, of course, run along," said Grandmother Defendov's toothless lips, while with fierce brows she fixed Liza in her place. Then she turned to her son.

"Poor little kid," she said, when the claret-coloured curtains had closed behind Zhenia.

A sombre complete set of *The North* bent one shelf down and on the bottom shelf was the dull gold of the complete works of Karamzin. A pink lantern hanging from the ceiling failed to light up a couple of threadbare little arm-chairs, and a small rug lost in the utter darkness was a surprise to her feet.

Zhenia had thought she was going to go into that room, sit down and burst into sobs. But though tears come to her eyes they could not break through her grief. How was she ever to roll away the barrier which last night's misery had put there? Tears would not come and she was powerless to remove the obstruction. To assist her tears she turned her thoughts to her mother.

For the first time in her life, now she was about to spend the night in a strange house she measured the depth of her attachment to that dear person, most precious thing in all the world.

Suddenly, through the curtains, she heard Liza's loud laughter.

"Oh, you little imp, you . . ."

And Grandmother Defendov coughed and rocked to and fro. Zhenia was astounded to think she had once thought she loved that girl whose laughter was ringing out in the next room but who was so far from her, meant nothing to her. And something in her turned right over and let the tears come at the same instant as her mother came back to her, suffering, lost away back there in the long chain of yesterday's events, which was like a crowd of people seeing her off, dizzily seen in the far distance as the train of time swept Zhenia away from her.

That keen look that her mother had fixed on her the day before in the class-room was absolutely, absolutely unbearable. It had cut deep into her mind and would not leave it, and everything Zhenia was now going through became part of it. As if it were a thing she ought to have taken and kept great care of, but had been scorned and forgotten.

She might have lost her head altogether through that feeling, its intoxicating demented bitterness and inevitability played such havoc with her, and she stood by the window and wept copiously and silently, letting the tears flow unwiped, her hands not being free to touch them, though those hands were doing nothing else, merely stretched out, tense and strong and stubborn and straight.

Then a sudden thought dazzled her. She all at once felt how *terribly* like her mother she was. This feeling merged into a sensation of living infallibility capable of transforming concept into reality by the mere force of that staggeringly sweet state of resemblance. The sensation pierced her through and through till she could have cried from the pain of it. *It was the sensation of a woman inwardly or from within perceiving her own external nature and charm.* Zhenia could not cope with it; this was the very first time she had experienced it.

She went back to the Defendovs drunk from tears, but illumined, and she walked now with another walk, not her own, but with broad, dreamily straddling steps. When she saw her come in Mr Defendov felt at once that the idea he had formed of this little girl while she was out of the room did not fit, and had the samovar not engaged his attention he would have formed a new one.

Mrs Defendov went out to the kitchen for a tray, leaving the samovar on the floor, all eyes fixed on the smoking copper as if it was a live creature, whose miserable waywardness was bound to cease the instant it was lifted back on to the table. Zhenia went back to her place. She made up her mind now to talk to everybody. She had a vague feeling that after this it was for her to choose the topic of conversation, or they would keep her for ever in the isolated state she had been in before, and not see that her mother was there with her, in her. Such shortsightedness would hurt her, and, what was more, would hurt her Mummy. And as if her mother were really there to encourage her, she turned to Mrs Defendov, who was with some difficulty edging the samovar on to the tray.

"Vassa Vassilievna . . ." she said like, any other grown-up.

.   .   .   .   .

"And can you have babies?"

Liza did not answer Zhenia at once.

"Shh! Don't shout, silly!" Then: "Why, of course I can, like all other girls."

This was said in a jerky jumpy whisper. Zhenia could not see her friend's face. Liza was feeling about on the table, but could not find the matches.

She knew a lot more about all that than Zhenia did. In fact, she knew *everything*—just as do all children who learn of such things from chance words dropped here and there. And then all those natures which are favourites of their maker rise in revolt and indignation and become wild. Through this trial they cannot pass without pathology. It would be completely unnatural otherwise. Childish madness at this age is merely the seal of profound normality.

One day Liza had heard a string of foolish stuff and dirty nonsense about those matters whispered furtively. Liza did not turn a hair, but kept it all close in her mind and carried it home. Not a detail of it did she lose on the way home, but preserved the whole mass of rubbish. She found out everything. There was no conflagration in her organism, no tocsin was sounded by her heart, nor was there any attack by soul on brain for daring to learn anything on the sly like that, apart from her, not from her own lips, her soul, but without asking.

"I know too."

('No you don't know anything at all,' said Liza to herself.)

"I know," Zhenia repeated, "I'm not asking about that.

58

What I want to know is, do you ever feel as if, if you took just one more step, you'd have a baby at once?"

"Do come inside," Liza cried in a hoarse voice, stifling her laughter. "Fine place you pick to shout. Why, they could hear you, standing in the doorway."

This conversation took place in Liza's room. Liza spoke so quietly that Zhenia could hear the water dripping from the tap. She had found the matches now, but she did not want to light the lamp for a moment, as she could not at once screw up her grinning cheeks into a serious expression. She did not want to hurt her friend's feelings. And she had mercy on Zhenia's ignorance because she was unable to imagine talking about those things in any other way but using expressions which she could not use at home, let alone in front of a friend who did not go to school.

Then she lit the lamp. Luckily the bucket had filled and ran over, so Liza hastily turned to wiping up the floor and hid a new fit of giggles in her pinafore and the swishing of her mop till at last there was an excuse and she could laugh out loud. Her comb had fallen into the bucket.

    .   .   .   .   .

All the while she was there Zhenia had only one thought— of her own people—and constantly longed for the hour when they would send for her. And to that end, every afternoon, when Liza was at school and she was alone in the house with Grandmother Defendov, Zhenia too dressed and went out alone to stretch her legs.

The life of that hamlet on the outskirts of the town was little like the life of any of the places where the Lüvers had ever lived. Most of the day it was deserted and dull. There was nothing for one's eye to dwell on. There was nothing to look at but material for birch rods or brooms. There was coal lying about. People simply tipped their dirty slops out into the street, where they immediately turned white, freezing. At certain hours of the day the street did fill with people, common people. The factory workers swarmed over the snow like beetles. The

doors of the tea-houses ran on rollers and soapy steam poured
out of them like out of wash-houses. Strange, but it seemed
somehow warmer in the street, as if they were getting round to
spring again, when those sodden peasant shirts hurried stooping
by, the felt slippers at the end of their thin trousers twinkling.
The pigeons showed no fear of those crowds, but flew down the
road for the food which was there. Was there not enough oats
and barley and horse droppings littering the snow? The
meat-pie woman's stall gleamed with grease and warmth,
and that grease and that warmth disappeared down cheap-
brandy bespattered throats. The grease brought fire to them,
and then, on the way back, it came out of those fast-breathing
chests. Was it that perhaps that warmed the street?

Just as suddenly it would be empty again, as dusk came
down. Peasant sleighs went home empty, and low sleighs
raced by with bearded men lost in fur coats and all laughter,
bodies rolling back and embracing each other like bears.
They left behind them little wisps of sad hay and the sweet
endless melting of their sleigh bells. Shopkeepers vanished
round the corner beyond the birches, which from where Zhenia
was, looked like a ragged stockade.

And this was where those crows came who flew over their
house with that untrammelled cawing. Only here they did not
caw. Here they called a halt to cawing, tucked in their wings,
and squatted on fences and then, all of a sudden, as if at some
sign, swept off in a cloud to master the trees and jostling
one another settle about those vacated branches. Ah, how
clearly then she could feel what a late hour it was in the
whole wide world! Such lateness as no clock face could ever
tell you!

.   .   .   .   .

Thus a week passed, and towards the end of the second
week, at daybreak on the Thursday, she saw him again.
Liza's bed was empty. Waking, Zhenia heard the wicket-gate
clatter to behind her. She got up and went to the window
without lighting the lamp. It was still quite dark. But she
could sense that in the sky and the branches of the trees and

the movements of the dogs there was the same heaviness that there had been the previous day. This was the third day of that overcast weather, and there was no more the strength to drag it off the dilapidated street than to drag a heavy iron saucepan off a rough shelf.

In a window opposite a lamp was lit. Two bright shafts of light pointed under the horse's belly and illuminated shaggy fetlocks. Shadows moved about the snow, and the arms of a ghostly figure wrapping its fur coat round it moved, and the light in the curtained window moved. But the little nag stood motionless, asleep.

Then she saw who it was. She knew him at once by his outline. The limping man took up a lantern and walked away with it. At his heels went two shafts of light, tipping to one side or other, lengthening and shortening, and behind them the sleigh, which swiftly flashed into sight and swifter still plunged back into darkness as it slowly went round the house to the front porch.

Strange that Tzvetkov should still come across her path here, in this hamlet outside the town. Yet it did not surprise Zhenia. She was not really interested in him. Soon the lantern appeared again and moved steadily past all the curtains, then started back again, and then all at once was on the window-sill behind the same curtain, where it had started.

This was Thursday. And on Friday, at last, they sent for her.

IX

When, ten days after her return home, and more than a three-weeks' break, lessons were resumed, Zhenia learned all the rest from her tutor. After dinner the doctor got ready and left, and she asked him to give her greetings to the house in which he had attended her that spring, and to all the streets, and to the River Kama. He expressed a hope that there would be no more need to send to Perm for him. She went to the gate with this man who had given her such shudders the very first morning when, after coming back from the Defendovs, while

61

Mummy was asleep and nobody was allowed into her room, in answer to her question, what was wrong with Mummy, he had begun by reminding her that *that* night Daddy and Mummy had gone to the theatre. And that after the play, as the people were coming out, their cob . . .

"Vykormysh?"

"Yes, if that's what you call him . . . well, Vykormysh, then, got restive and reared and knocked down and crushed a man who happened to be passing . . ."

"What? Killed him?"

"Unfortunately, yes."

"And Mummy?"

"Mummy had a bad shock," and he smiled, having scarcely thought in time of that way of adapting his Latin *partus praematurus* to a little girl's ears.

"And then my dead little brother was born?"

"Who told you? . . . Yes."

"But when? Were they there? Or did they find him already dead? Don't tell me. Oh, how terrible. Now I understand. He was already dead, or I should have heard him even if they had not been there. Because I was reading. Late that night. I should have heard. But when exactly did he live? Doctor, are such things possible? I even went into the bedroom. He was dead. There was no doubt about it."

How lucky that what she had seen from the Defendovs' house, at dawn, had been only last night, and that horror at the theatre three weeks ago! What luck she had recognised him. So much was clear to her—that if she had not seen him at all, after what the doctor had now told her she would have been sure to conclude that it was *he* who had been crushed at the theatre. And so, having spent so much time there and become quite one of the family, the doctor left.

That evening her tutor came. It had been washing day, and in the kitchen they were mangling the linen. Hoar-frost dropped off her shoulders, and the garden pressed close to the panes and wrapped itself in the lace curtains and came right up to the table. The jerky rumble of the mangle kept forcing its way into the conversation. Dikikh, like everybody else, found her changed. For that matter, she could see a change in him too.

"Why are you so sad?"

"Am I? Everything's possible. A friend of mine has died."

"You have something to grieve about too? What a lot of deaths—and all at once!"

She sighed.

But just as he was about to tell her what sort of a friend he had had, something quite unexpected happened. She suddenly had quite a different view of the number of those who had died, and, evidently forgetting what support she possessed in the lantern she had seen that very morning, was terribly upset and said:

"Wait a moment. One day you went to the tobacconist, the day Negarat left, and I saw you with someone else. Was it him?" She was afraid to say 'Was it Tzvetkov?'

Dikikh was taken aback when he heard what she said. He thought back and recalled that indeed they had gone to buy a paper about that time and tried to buy a complete Turgeniev for Mrs Lüvers, and it was true his dead friend had been with him. She shuddered and tears sprang to her eyes. But the principal thing was yet to come.

When, with breaks filled by the rumbling of the mangle, Dikikh had told her what a fine young fellow his friend had been, and of what a good family, and at last lit a cigarette, Zhenia was horrified to see that now only this brief delay still separated her from a repetition of the doctor's story, and when at last Dikikh tried and had got out a few words, including the word *theatre*, Zhenia suddenly shrieked and rushed out of the room, beside herself.

Dikikh listened carefully. There was not a sound in the house but the rumble of the mangle. He rose to his feet, just like a stork. He stretched out his neck and raised one foot, preparing to rush to her aid. He made off to find her, being sure nobody else was at home, and she had gone mad. And while he was stumbling in the dark, feeling at puzzles of wood, wool and metal, Zhenia was sitting huddled in a corner sobbing. Dikikh went on fumbling round and searching, in thought already

63

raising her dead body from the floor. He started violently when at his elbow he suddenly heard a low sob-broken voice cry loudly:

"I'm here. Do be careful, there's a whatnot right beside you. Wait for me in the class-room. I'll be there in a minute."

The curtains reached the floor and the starry winter night outside also swept the floor, and, waist-deep in the drifts, the low drowsy trees dragged their chains of bare branches through the deep snow towards the bright spot of light in the window. And somewhere on the other side of the wall, taut with sheets, the hard rumble of the mangle persisted. And the tutor puzzled—how was one to explain that sudden outburst of over-sensitivity? Clearly the dead man occupied some very special place in this child's estimation. She had changed so much. He had been explaining recurring decimals to a little girl, whereas this young woman who had just sent him to the class-room. . . . And that was the work of one month? Obviously the deceased had some time or other made a particularly powerful, an ineffaceable impression on her. . . . Impressions of that sort had a name. How extraordinary it all was. He had given her lessons every other day and had never noticed anything. She was a *frightfully nice* kid, and he was terribly sorry for her. But when on earth would she get that cry over and come to him? The whole household must be out. 'I really am sorry for her. What a remarkable night!'

He was mistaken. The kind of impression he was thinking of did not fit the case at all. He was not mistaken. The impression at the bottom of it all was indeed one that never could be erased. But it was far deeper down than he thought. . . . It was beyond the girl's own knowing, because it was vitally important and significant, and its significance consisted in this being the first time that *another person*, a stranger, had intruded in her life, and it was of no account who this was, or what name the person had, or that neither hatred nor love were aroused; *it was the same person that you get in the imperative form of a verb* concerning precise names and concepts, when people said: thou shalt not steal, and all the rest. Such commandments say: 'You, you, particular living individual, do not do to

64

hazy generalized person anything that you, particular living person, do not wish to be done to yourself.' Dikikh's most clumsy error of all was in thinking that impressions of that kind have a name. They have not.

As for her tears, they were because Zhenia felt she was herself to blame for it all. Was she not responsible for introducing that person into the life of the family that day by seeing him across the garden, and, once having thus noticed him, for coming upon him, without need to or purpose or point, constantly, directly and indirectly, even, as happened on that last occasion, contrary to all probability?

When she saw which book Dikikh was taking from the shelves she frowned and said:

'No. I won't do that today. Put it back. Please excuse me.'

And, without another word, the same hand that took them out pushed Lermontov's poems back into the little lop-sided row of classics.

Il Tratto Di Apelle

> . . . Legend has it that the Greek painter
> Apelles, calling one day on his rival,
> Zeuxis, and not finding him at home,
> drew a brush mark on the wall by which
> Zeuxis knew who had been in his absence.
> Zeuxis returned tit for tat. Choosing an
> hour when he was sure he would not find
> Apelles at home, he too left his mark,
> now famous in the world of painting.

I

On one of those September evenings when the leaning tower
of Pisa leads a whole army of leaning sunsets and leaning
shadows up the slopes to attack the city, when from the whole
of Tuscany, wind-fretted to fury, is wafted the odour of bay
leaves rubbed between the fingers, on such an evening, why,
what nonsense, I remember the very date, it was August the
twenty-third—that evening, when he called at the inn and
found Heine out, Emilio Relinquimini requested the cringing
service porter to provide him with paper and a light. The man
did better. He brought ink too, together with pen and stick of
sealing-wax and seal. But with scornful gesture Relinquimini
waved him aside. Drawing out the pin which held his tie, he
heated this to red heat in the candle-flame, then, jabbing it
into his finger, snatched one of the packet of correspondence
cards printed with the hotel address, and with the pricked
finger-tip bent back one corner. Handing this to the utterly
unmoved but ever-obsequious hotel porter, he said:

"Give Mr Heine this visiting card. I shall call again tomorrow,
at the same hour."

The leaning tower of Pisa forced a passage through the cordon of medieval fortifications. The number of people watching it from the bridge increased with every minute. Sunsets—partisan sunsets—crept across the squares. The streets were barricaded with overthrown shadows. In the narrower alleys there was still fighting, shadows hacking one another down. Careless of safety, backwards leant the tower of Pisa, till a giant shadow crept over the sun itself. . . . And day snapped off. Nevertheless, while there were still seconds to run before complete sunset with brief, broken phrases the hotel porter contrived to inform *Signor* Heine of his recent visitor and hand the impatient hotel guest the card with the dried-up, already darkening blot on it.

"Well, what an eccentric!"

Heine however was not slow to guess his visitor's real name. It was the author of the famous poem *Blood—Il sangue*.

The coincidence by which the Ferraran Reliquinini should happen to be in Pisa precisely when the still more accidental whim of the wandering poet Heine the Westphalian brought him to this town, did not seem strange to the German poet. To his mind at once came the anonymous person who had recently sent him that carelessly scrawled, challenging letter. The claim put forward by that stranger really went too far. After some hazy, oblique phrases about the aristocratic, pure-blooded roots of poetry, the unknown correspondent had requested Heine to furnish him with a proof of identity in the style of Apelles. Love, the stranger wrote, that sanguinary wall of mists which can only temporarily befog our otherwise unclouded blood—"well, make some pronouncement about that passion such that your jotting does not exceed the laconic stroke of Apelles' brush in brevity! Do not forget, the only thing your Zeuxis is inquisitive about is to what degree you really do belong to the aristocracy of blood and spirit (inseparable concepts).

"P.S. I have taken advantage of your stay in Pisa, of which I was informed in good time by my publisher, Conti, once and for all time to bring the doubts which torment me to an end.

In three days' time I will call on you again to view your Apelles' mark."

The hotel servant who appeared at Heine's summons was met point-blank with the following instructions from the guest:

"I am catching the ten o'clock train to Ferrara. Tomorrow evening the gentleman with whom you are already familiar— the visitor who left this card—will ask for me. You will hand him this letter. Please let me have my bill at once. And call a *facchino*."

The wraith-like absence of weight with which the apparently empty envelope was endowed it owed to a very, very thin little slip of paper, clearly scissored out of a manuscript work, a fragment embracing two phrases out of the very heart of a sentence:

". . . but, discarding their former names, he crying 'Rondolfina!' she breathing: 'Oh! Enrico!', Rondolfina and Enrico contrived to assume others, which had never before been used."

II

On the paving stones and the asphalt of the squares, on balconies and on the Arno embankments, the Pisans consumed the sweet-odoured Tuscan night. That murky fire made the narrow alleys under the dusty plane trees, stifling enough at best, still more oppressive, and in addition to the sultry, oily gleam of that conflagration were added the grain-shedding sheaves of the stars and those tufts of spiny cloud. And those cinders filled the cup of patience of the Italians brimful. Cursing with fanatical fire, as if uttering prayers, and merely glancing at Cassiopeia, they wiped the dusty perspiration from their foreheads. Their handkerchiefs waved in the darkness like clinical thermometers being shaken down. The indications which those cambric scales gave swept most depressingly through the streets. They spread the stuffiness far and wide, like eavesdropped rumours, like an epidemic, like panic terror. And just as without resistance that leaning city fell apart into wards, courtyards and houses, so too did the night air turn to disparate immobilised meetings, to exclamations, disputes, sanguinary clashes, whispers, scorn and denunciations.

All these sounds lay close-laced and dusty in regular ranks about the pavement, taking root in the footwalks, like avenue trees breathless and colourless in gaslight. Thus in its whimsical, wilful way did that Pisan night rigorously ring off the contours of man's tolerance. And, but a handsbreadth beyond, there began chaos. Chaos which reigned at the railway station. Where handkerchiefs and curses *exeunt*.

Those who a moment before had considered natural locomotion all but torture here hauled suitcases and holdalls, jostled at the ticket-offices and charged stampeding at sooty railway coaches, storming the steps, forcing their smut-stained way like chimney-sweeps, into compartments walled off with hot dun panelling which seemed to be warping from the heat and the swearing and that terrible battering. And the coaches blazed, the rails below them blazed, the petroleum tanks blazed and the locomotives in the sidings, the signals blazed and the steam-engulfed, flat-squashed howls of the locomotives far and near swollen with steam also blazed. Tiptoeing slow on spurts of steam, like a snorting insect the slow locomotive spat the overpowering breath of its open furnace on to the driver's cheeks and the fireman's leather tunic. The clock face burned, the cast-steel reverberation of the shunting rails and switches burned. It was all beyond the limits of human endurance. But yet all could be borne.

· · · · · ·

A window seat. At the final moment absolutely empty, there was the solid stone platform, there the solid stone sonority, the solid stone cry of the conductor: *"Pronti!— All away!"* And he raced past the window, chasing his own voice. With dignity the station columns swept by. Like knitting needles lights twinkled out and intercrossed. Bright station lights flashed in at the train windows, the draught caught swiftly at them and swept them through the compartment and out on the other side, and there the iron rails caught at them and stretched them out. And they stumbled on the rails and picked themselves up again, to vanish at last behind the station sheds. Dwarf alleys, freakish mongrel little offcourts. Blustering right up to the blinds of onsweeping gardens. Relaxed spaciousness of curly carpets of vineyards. Open country.

Travelling blind, Heine, with vacant head. Heine trying to lose himself for a moment in sleep. Heine closing his eyes.

'No doubt something will come of this. No sense in trying now to imagine what—impossible, indeed. Ahead I have complete uncertainty. So encouraging.'

Oranges, no doubt, in bloom. The sweet-scented expanse of gardens, overflowing. Whence was wafted a faint air breath, to absorb be it but one bead of moisture from the traveller's glueing lashes.

It was a certainty. Something would come of it. And how delightful too—*aaa-ah* (Heine yawning)—how delightful too any love poem of Relinquimini's would be, with that reliable trade-mark: Ferrara!

Crags, precipices, fellow-travellers sleep-broken, train reek, and the flickering light of the gas. From the ceiling licking the rustle and the shadows, then with a sigh licking its lips as the crags and the precipices surrendered to a tunnel and thundering the massif grazed the train's roof and the engine smoke was rolled to a ribbon, which clutched at the hooks and the luggage rack and drove Heine back from the window. Tunnels and valleys. The single-track line moaned mournfully over the mountain stream which broke on rocks as in darkness it came tumbling down from incredible peaks that gleamed faintly in the darkness. And there above were waterfalls, sootily smoking, all through the night their dull roar wrapping round the train.

'The brush-stroke of Apelles . . . Rondolfina . . .' Surely one day would not be enough. Yet that was the limit.

'I must vanish without trace. Whereas tomorrow . . . the moment he finds out from the hotel where I have gone, he will rush to the station!'

Ferrara! Blue-black, steely dawn. Sweet-scented coolth-soaked mist. O sonority of a dawn in Latium!

III

"Impossible, the next issue of *Voce* is already made up for press."

"Maybe, but on no account, not for any money in the world, will I hand over my finds. Not to anybody in the world. Nor can I stay in Ferrara more than a day."

"In the train, you say, under the seat? His diary?"

"Yes, Emilio Relinquimini's diary! What's more, a diary which, among a mass of day-to-day jottings, also contains a great quantity of unpublished verse, a number of drafts of poems, short notes and aphorisms. A whole year's diary, in fact, mainly written, as far as one can tell by his remarks, here in Ferrara!"

"Where is it? Have you brought it with you?"

"Oh no! I left all my things at the station. The diary is locked in my luggage."

"Now, what a pity! We might have delivered it at once to his house. We have his Ferrara address in the office files—though for that matter, he has been away for the past month."

"Do you mean to assert that Relinquimini is not in Ferrara?"

"That's just the point. So I really cannot quite grasp what you hope to gain by putting an announcement of your find in the paper."

"All I hope is to be able to do—through your paper—is to make sure of meeting the owner of the diary. Surely Relinquimini should at any time be able to count on the courtesy of *Voce* in such a matter?"

"How persistent you are, sir! Pray be seated. Perhaps you would kindly write out the little advertisement you have in mind."

"I am sorry indeed to be such a great nuisance, but may I use your phone a moment?"

"Why, of course you may. At your service!"

"Hello! Is that the *Albergo Torquato Tasso*? Yes? Can you tell me if you have any room left? On which floor? Excellent, then I'll take *Number eight*."

FOUND: Text, prepared for printer, of new book by Emilio Relinquimini. Will the owner or his representative call up to 11 p.m. on the occupant of Room No. 8 in the *Albergo Torquato Tasso*, who will be expecting him. From tomorrow on the Editorial Office of *Voce* and the management of the *Albergo* in question will regularly and in good time be informed by the advertiser of every change in his address.

Tired from his journey, Heine slept like a log. At last, warmed by the breath of morning, the Venetian blinds of his room glowed like the brass reeds of a mouth-organ. Under the window a network of the sun's rays spread across the floor like a straw mat. Pressing close, hugging one another, the blades of straw all ran together. Outside, indecipherable talking began, a man getting so excited that he was quite tongue-tied.

An hour passed. By now the blades of straw had fused and the mat had turned into a pool of sunshine. Outside, the talkers were getting excited, pecking at each other, till they were quite tongue-tied.

Heine slept on. The pool of sunlight grew emaciated, as if soaking into the parquet flooring. Again it was a mat growing thinner, a mat made of straw stalks, pleated and smouldering.

Heine slept on. Talking outside. Hours passing, hours idly springing up, hours growing longer, like the black gaps between the straws of the mat.

Talking outside. The mat began to fade. The mat became dusty. The mat grew dull. Now but a string mat tossed, tumbled there, weft and woof and knotting all indistinguishable. And talking outside.

And Heine asleep.

Any moment, now, the awakening. At any moment now Heine will leap to his feet—mark my words! At any moment. Only let him see his dream out to the end. . . .

Dried out by the heat, the wheel suddenly split to the very nave, fanning its out-thrust spokes, a quiver of cut spikes, the little wagon shattered clattering, lurching to one side. Bundles of newspapers tipped out—crowds, parasols, shop windows, marquises—stretcher-borne, the delivery boy. Only a stone's throw away, a dispensing chemist's.

You see! What did I say?

Heine leaps to his feet.

"Just a moment!"

At the door, somebody knocking, impatiently, wildly knocking.

Tousled and bleary and dreamy, Heine grabs at his gown.

"So sorry, just a moment!"

With almost metallic clank, right foot, to the floor.

"Just a moment. Ah, there we are!"

Heine goes to the door.

"Who is there?"

An hotel porter's voice.

"Yes, yes, I have the diary. Please ask the *Signora* to excuse me a moment. Is she in the lounge?"

The man's voice.

"Please ask the *Signorina* if she could possibly wait about ten minutes. In ten minutes' time I shall be entirely at her service. Do you hear me?"

The man's voice.

"Wait a moment, *cameriere*!"

The man's voice.

"Don't forget to tell *Mademoiselle* that the *Signor* expresses his unlimited regret that he is unable to come to her immediately, he feels most guilty, but he will endeavour—are you listening, *cameriere*?"

The man's voice.

73

"He will endeavour in ten minutes' time to erase his unforgivable neglect to the full. Only, *cameriere*, please, be as courteous as you can. After all, I am not a Ferraran."

The man's voice.

"Very well, very well."

"*Cameriere*, have you shown the lady into the lounge?"

"Yes, *Signor*."

"Is she alone there?"

"Alone, *Signor*. Waiting for you, *Signor*. The first door on the left, *Signor*. On the left."

"Good afternoon. How may I be at your service, *Madame*?"

"Are you the gentleman staying in room number eight, sir?"

"I am that person."

"I have come to fetch Mr Relinquimini's diary."

"Allow me to introduce myself. I am Heinrich Heine."

"I beg your pardon, sir. . . . Are you any relation . . . to . . . er?"

"Not in the least. Purely coincidental, my name. Rather embarrassing, indeed. . . . Because I, too . . ."

"You are a poet, too?"

"I have never written anything else."

"I know German and poetry is my great relaxation, but yet . . ."

"Do you happen to know a little book called *Lines Never Published During the Poet's Lifetime*?"

"But of course I do. So you are the author of that, are you?"

"Forgive me, it is my great aspiration to learn your name."

"I am Camilla Ardenze."

"I am most enchanted. . . . So you noticed my advertisement in today's *Voce*, did you, *Signora* Ardenze?"

"But of course. About this diary you have found. Where is it? Will you let me have it, please?"

"*Signora! Signora* Camilla! Perhaps with all that heart of yours, which the incomparable Relinquinini has enshrined in verse——"

"That, *Signor* Heine, is quite enough. *We* are not on the stage——"

"*Signora*, you are mistaken, all our life we are on the stage, though rare the person who can achieve that naturalness of performance with which we are each of us endowed at birth.

"*Signora* Camilla, you love your native city, you love Ferrara. Yet this is the first town that definitely repels me. You, however, are lovely, *Signora* Camilla, and my heart shrinks at the mere notion that you should be in secret connivance with this city, against myself."

"I simply do not understand——"

"*Signora*, do not interrupt me. With the town, I was saying, that drugged me so, just as a poisoner drugs his bottle companion, when his happiness brings him to the poisoner, drugging him in order to stir up a spark of scorn for the poor man in the eyes of that happiness when she comes to the tavern, whereupon happiness deceives the drugged one. '*Milady*,' says the poisoner to the woman who enters, 'just look at this idle fellow! This is the man you have lavished your love on. He whiled away his time of waiting with stories of you, and their spurs speared my imagination. I suppose you rode here on its back? Why did you lash it so mercilessly with your slender crop? It is all in a lather, it is over-heated.

" 'Oh, those stories! But try not to look at him. *Milady*, he has been drugged to sleep by his own stories about you—see for yourself, absence from you works like a lullaby on your beloved! Yet we can waken him.' 'You should not,' comes the reply of the poisoned man's happiness to the poisoner. 'Don't, do not disturb him,' it says, 'he is sleeping so sweetly, perhaps he is even dreaming about me. Far better find me a glass of good toddy. It is so cold outside. I am frozen through. Please massage my hands for me . . .' "

"You are a very strange person, Mr Heine. But please go on, I find your high fancy intriguing."

"Sorry, so long as you don't forget about Relinquimini's diary. I'll run up to my room. . . ."

"Please don't worry, I shall not forget that. Do go on. How interesting you are! Do please continue. Massage my hands for me — which, I gather, was uttered by happiness?"

75

"That is so, *Signora* Camilla. You have been most attentive. Thank you."

"And so?"

"Well, just that this city has treated me as the poisoner the man who drank in his company, and you, lovely Camilla, you are on its side. It eavesdropped on my thoughts of dawns ancient and crumbling as bandits' castles and as lonely, and it drugged me so as slily to use them and have me babble about galleons under full sail from the scarlet air of evening fast running out to the open night, and so, you see, unfurled those sails, but left me sprawling in the harbour tavern, and here are you, the moment the crafty rascal so suggests to you, refusing to let it waken me."

"My dear man, come, come, do please explain what I have to do with all this. Or did the hotel servant not really quite waken you up?"

"No, you will say, night's drawing nigh, lest there's a storm, we must hurry, it's high time, don't waken him."

"Ah, *Signor* Heine, how profoundly mistaken you are! Why, what I will say is, yes, yes, Ferrara, shake him up, if he's still asleep, I've no time to spare, waken him as quickly as you can, gather all your crowds, make all your squares re-echo, till at last you do waken him, utterly, there's no time to be lost."

"Yes, of course, that diary . . . ! "

"After, after . . ."

"Ah, dear *Signora*, Ferrara has made a great miscalculation. Ferrara is fooled, the poisoner's in flight, I am waking, I am utterly awake—on my knees at your feet! My love!"

Camilla Ardenze leapt to her feet.

"Enough! Enough! True, it all suits you well. Even the well-worn phrases. Especially the well-worn phrases. But you really must not, you know! Why, you are merely a wandering play-actor. We scarcely know one another. It was only half an hour ago . . . Yes, Good Heavens! I find it funny even to think of it —and yet—and yet I am discussing it, you see. I never felt so silly in all my life before. This whole scene, just like a Japanese flower, opening up the moment it touches water. Neither more

nor less. But do remember, they are only paper flowers. And
so cheap!"

"I am all attention, *Signora*."

"*Signor*, I would rather listen to you. You are very wise,
even sarcastic, I rather think. And yet not afraid of stooping
to well-worn phrases. Strange, yet not contradictory. Your
histrionic pathos . . ."

"Pardon me, *Signora*, but *pathos* is a Greek word, in the
original signifying passion, but in Italian only a blown kiss.
Perforce kisses so light . . ."

"Again, sir! I must declare, this is insufferable! You have
some secret purpose. Please explain yourself! But please, my
dear Mr Heine, do not be angry with me. In spite of it all you—
you will not be annoyed with me if I am outspoken?—you are
a most weird—er—child. No, even that is not quite the right
word. Yes—you are a poet. Of course! However did I fail to
find the words at once, all one need do is take one look at you.
One of Providence's chosen idlers, a spoiled child of—good
fortune."

"*Evviva!*"

Crying this, Heine leapt lightly to the window-sill and leant
far out.

"Oh, do be careful, *Signor* Heine!" cried Camilla. "Do
please be careful, I am so afraid for you!"

"You need not fear, dear *Signora*."

"Oh, *furfante* [rascal]! Catch!"

Liras fly out, into the square.

"There, you'll get as much, even ten times the amount, if
you plunder as many Ferrara gardens. A *soldo* for every hole
in your trousers. Off with you! Only take care, when you bring
in the flowers, don't breathe on them, the countess has the
sensitivity of mimosa. Off with you, mountebank!"

"Enchantress, did you hear? The lad will come back attired
as a cupid. Well, to business. But what perspicacity! By one
stroke of the brush, one stroke of Apelles, to reveal my whole
self, the very essence of the situation."

"I don't understand you. Or is this a fresh way out? More
histrionics? Or what exactly is it you want?"

"Yes, histrionics again. Yet why not let me spend a few moments under the arc-lights' glare? After all, I am not to blame, am I, if in life it is the most dangerous sites that are most brilliantly lighted—the temporary planking, the gangways? What brilliance! All else is plunged in darkness."

On such boards—yes, even if they are the boards of a stage—a man catches alight, lit by uneasy fires, as if made an example for all, railed round with barriers, by the panorama of the city, with whirlpools and lighthouses.

"*Signora* Camilla, you would not give heed to half my words, had you and I not come together in so perilous a place. It is perilous. That we must assume, although I myself am not conscious of it. We must assume so because men have spent endless sums on fire to light it up, and it is not my fault if we are illuminated so crudely, so harshly."

"Very well, then. Have you finished? All you say is so. Yet, you know, it is all such incredible nonsense. I would like to trust you. No mere whim, that. Almost a necessity in me. You are not lying. Your eyes do not lie. Yes, but what now was it that I wanted to say to you . . . ? It has slipped from my mind. . . . Just a moment. . . . Ah, yes. . . . Listen, my dear friend—after all, only an hour since——"

"Stop! Mere words! There are hours and there are eternities. Very many but not one that has any beginning. They reveal themselves all at once, at the first favourable moment. And that is chance itself. And then—down with words! *Signora*, when and by whom are they overthrown? Down with words! Have you ever encountered such rebellions, *Signora*? *Signora*—all my fibres rise against me, and I am obliged to yield to them, as one yields to a crowd. And here is one final point: do you remember what you called me just now?"

"Of course I do. I am prepared to call you that a second time."

"You should not. Yet you are able to look with such life-giving force. And you are already master of a brush-stroke as unique as life itself. Only do not let it slip from your grasp, do not load it either on to me, hold it back as long as it will let you. Take that line farther away.

78

"What is the result, *Signora*? How have you come out? Side-view? Or three-quarters? Or, if neither, how?"

"I see what you mean."

Camilla held out her hand to Heine.

"And all the same . . . No, Good Heavens, I am not a mere schoolgirl. I must pull myself together. This is like hypnosis."

"*Signora*," cried Heine, theatrically, now at Camilla's feet. "*Signora!*" he repeated, in a choking voice, hiding his face in his hands. "Have you finished your brush-stroke?"

"Oh, what torture!" half whispering, he gasped, tearing his hands away from his cheeks, which had suddenly become bloodless. . . . And then, peering into the eyes of *Signora* Ardenze, who was more and more losing her self-control, to his inexpressible amazement he observed that . . .

IV

. . . that this woman was indeed beautiful, beautiful beyond conception, that the beating of his own heart, which was like seas surging in the wake of a ship, was growing in strength, breaking now over knees drawing ever nearer and in slow high-piling waves flooding over her body, about her silks lapping, drawing deep and still over her shoulders, till it reached her chin and, in wonder, was raising it slightly higher, raising it higher still, till this *signora* was up to the throat in his heart, and one more such wave and she would be utterly drowned there. And Heine seized the drowning woman—a kiss, and what a kiss, a kiss which, even though it groaned a great groan from the strain of their wild, pulsating hearts, swept them both off their feet, plucking them up and soaring with them into far distant, lofty spaces, no matter whither, merely to be away, away, and she made no resistance, oh none at all. Indeed, her kiss-drawn, kiss-compelled, kiss-ecstatic body, sang—if you will then I an argosy shall be of such kissing, only to be borne away, she borne away, me borne away!

"Somebody's . . . knocking!" hoarsely broke from Camilla's breast.

"Somebody's knocking!"
And she tore from his embrace.
And she was right.

.   .   .   .   .

"A thousand devils! Who's that?"
"*Signor*, you should not lock the lounge door. It is not permitted."
"Hold your tongue! I can do as I please."
"You are ill, sir."
Oaths, passionate, fantastic Italian oaths, like a liturgical rite. Heine unlocked the door. In the corridor stood an hotel servant, still muttering. Behind him, a few paces back, was a young lad, very ragged, his head lost in an absolute jungle of jasmine and branches of oleander and orange-blossom and lilies . . .
"This rascal . . .
. . . and roses and magnolia blossom and carnations. . . .
"This rascal . . . tried to insist on being allowed into the room with windows facing the square, the only such room being the lounge . . ."
"Yes, yes, into the lounge," cried this bull-voiced, guttural whipper-snapper.
"Of course, into the lounge," Heine agreed. "Those were my own instructions to him."
". . . because," the hotel servant resumed, impatiently, "he could have no business in the office, or the bathrooms, let alone in the library. However, considering the completely unsuitable condition of his attire . . ."
"Oh yes, of course!" cried Heine, as if he had only this moment woken up. "Rondolfina, just look at his trousers! Whoever made those trousers for you, from fish-net, you transparent creature?"
"*Signor*, the prickly thorns of the Ferrara hedges are trimmed every year by seasonal gardeners."
"Ha, ha, ha!"
". . . Seeing the completely unsuitable condition of his

attire," the hotel servant now impatiently resumed, and he lent special emphasis to the word *attire* because of the *signora*'s joining them, her features clouded with sudden incomprehension struggling with rays of utterly irrepressible gaiety, ". . . seeing the completely unsuitable condition of his attire, we asked the lad to hand to us what the gentleman had ordered and wait for an answer outside. But the young scoundrel——"

"Yes, of course, he was quite right to insist"—Heine halted the eloquent fellow—"you see, I told him he was to present himself to the *Signorina* in person——"

". . . this young scoundrel," bellowed the hot-tempered Calabrian, completely losing control of himself, "began to utter threats."

"And what exactly did he threaten you with?" Heine enquired. "How picturesque, isn't it, *Signora?*"

"The ragged fellow referred us to you. The *Signor*, he threatened, the *Signor* is a business man and when he comes through Ferrara again he would make use of other hotels, if, in spite of the *Signor*'s orders, we did not allow the young rascal to go to him."

"Ha, ha, ha! What a funny fellow! Isn't he, *Signora?* Now take this tropical plantation away—no, wait"—and Heine turned to Camilla for her instructions. "Take it to room number eight, for the time being," he continued, without waiting for her answer.

"To your room, for the time being," Camilla repeated, blushing slightly.

"Very well, *Signor*. But as for this lad. . . ."

"Yes, you, you baboon, what price do you put on those trousers?"

"Giulio all scars, Giulio blue wiz cold, Giulio ha'n't got any other clothes, Giulio ha'n't got no dad, no mum," whined the ten-year-old young ragamuffin, coming out into a sweat.

"Well, hurry up, give me a straight answer; what price?"

"A hundred *soldi*, *Signor*," said the lad, hesitantly, dreamily, speaking like one mesmerized.

"Ha, ha, ha!"

Everybody guffawed. Heine guffawed, Camilla guffawed,

the hotel servant broke into guffaws, he in particular when, taking out his note-case, Heine pulled out a ten-lira note and, still laughing, handed it to the tatterdemalion.

Like a flash of lightning, out shot the boy's hand and snatched the money.

"Just a moment," Heine said. "I expect this is your first effort in commerce. Just in the nick of time. . . . Here, my man," he turned to the hotel servant, "let me assure you that in this case your laughter is definitely unseemly. It is wounding this young business man and, besides, am I not right, young man, in assuming that from now on in your business operations you will never again set foot in this inhospitable *albergo?*"

"But of course not, *Signor*, on the contrary. . . . But how many more days are you staying in Ferrara?"

"In two hours' time I leave this city for ever."

.   .   .   .   .   .

"*Signor* Enrico . . ."

"Yes, *Signora?*"

"Let us go outside, we surely are not going back into that stupid lounge?"

"Very well. . . . Boots—take these flowers up to number eight, will you? Just a moment, this rose still needs to open fully. For this evening the gardens of Ferrara consign it to you, *Signora.*"

"Thank you very much, Enrico. . . . And this swarthy carnation lacks any sense of self-control—*Signor*, the gardens of Ferrara consign this harum-scarum blossom to your care."

"Give me your dainty hand, *Signora*, to kiss! . . . So take these to number eight, my man. And bring me down my hat. You will find it in my room."

The man withdrew.

"Enrico, you will not do this."

"I do not quite follow, Camilla."

"You will stay on here? . . . Oh, please do not answer me back. . . . You will stay, won't you? At least for the day . . .

here in Ferrara. . . . Enrico, Enrico, you have dusted your forehead with pollen, let me brush it clean for you."

"*Signora* Camilla, I see a caterpillar on your shoe. . . . I will brush it off. I will telegraph home to Frankfort. And your frock is all petals, *Signora*—and I will go on telegraphing till you tell me not to."

"Enrico, I see there is no engagement ring on your finger. Have you ever put one on?"

"But on the other hand, long since I noticed that you wear one, Camilla. . . . Ah yes, my hat. Thank you."

V

The sweet-scented evening, penetrating into every corner of Ferrara, trickled in sonorous drops throughout the city's labyrinthine streets, just as a drop of sea-water, stealing its way into one's ear, fills one's whole head with deafness.

It was noisy in the café. But leading to it was a tiny alley which was silent and incorporeal, and the principal reason for this was that as the deafened, stupefied city enclosed it in, its tense walls held their breath. Thus evening sheltered in that narrow urban walk, in precisely this alley, with the café at the corner.

While she waited for Heine, Camilla began to wonder. He had gone to the telegraph office, which was next door to the café. Why, she wondered, had he so positively refused to write his telegram at the hotel and let a servant go to the post office to send it off? Surely it was not possible that he could not be content with a plain, formal message? Was it some very powerful bond, a bond of pure emotion? Yet, on the other hand, she recalled, he would have forgotten all about sending it, had she not reminded him. But whoever could Rondolfina be? She would have to ask him about that. But could she do so? After all, it would be a rather intimate question, wouldn't it?

'Good gracious,' she said to herself, 'I am just like a school-girl. I can, and I must. Today I acquire the right to anything, today I lose all rights. My dear girl, these actors have played havoc with you. But this one. . . . Then what about Relin-quimini? . . . How far-off his image! As far off as the Spring? Oh no, much farther off than that! A New Year's Eve? . . . But of course not, he was never really close to me. . . . Whereas this man? . . .'

"A penny for your thoughts, Camilla!"

"But why are you so downcast, Enrico? Don't you be sad: I release you. There are telegrams that hotel-servants can take down to dictation. Send one of those. You have only delayed your departure three hours. There is a night train to Venice and another night train to Milan. Your lateness will not exceed . . ."

"What is the point of all this, Camilla?"

"Why are you so downcast, Enrico? Now tell me something about Rondolfina."

With a violent start, Heine sprang to his feet.

"Who told you about Rondolfino? Is he here? He has been here in my absence!·Where is he, where is he, Camilla?"

"You are pale, Enrico. . . . And of whom do you speak? I was asking you about a woman—Rondolfina. Was I not? Or did I pronounce her name wrongly? Is it then Rondolfino? It all hangs on one vowel, doesn't it? Do sit down . . . people are staring."

"Who told you about her? Have you had news from him? But in what way? How did it get here? After all, we are in this place purely by chance, I mean, surely nobody *knows* we are here?"

"Enrico, nobody has been here and nothing whatever occurred while you were at the post office. I swear it. But with every minute the situation does become more curious. . . . So there are two such persons, are there?"

"Then it is a miracle! Beyond comprehension. . . . Utterly beyond me! Camilla, who put that name into your mind? Where did you first hear it?"

"Last night. In my sleep. Heavens, that is such an ordinary thing! But you still have not answered me: who exactly is this Rondolfina? Miracles have not vanished from the world—let us leave miracles alone—Enrico, who exactly is she?"

"Ah, Camilla, but of course, you are Rondolfina!"

"Oh, you false, lying pretender! No . . . no . . . let me be! Don't you dare touch me!"

They were now both on their feet. Camilla—with one movement—was transformed, to lightning, irrevocable agility. Only the café table was between them. She clutched the back of a chair as something rose up between her and her own decision, as something invaded her and the whole café, like roundabouts at the fair, whirled the whole place in a swirling wave, up, up, at an angle. . . . And fell, a victim. . . . Irresistible, that lance, in her body, for ever. . . .

All part of the queasy whirling furrow of the fair-world, with faces, wild concatenation, flowing past. . . . Spanish beards. . . . Monocles. . . . Opera glasses. . . . With every second ever more; all pointing at her. The talk at all tables pointed to theirs. She could still see him, she still resisting . . . this might pass off. . . . Not so the orchestra disjointed . . . off the beat. . . .

"Waiter, water!"

VI

Slightly feverish.

"What a tiny, tiny room yours is. . . . Yes, yes, that's just right, thank you. I'll lie still a little while longer. It's malaria— besides . . . I have a flat for us. But you should not leave me. It may break over me at any moment. Enrico!"

"Yes, darling?"

"Whyever are you so silent? No, no, don't, better so. . . . Oh, Enrico, I can't even remember whether there was any morning today. Are they still not falling?"

"Are what, Camilla?"

"The flowers."

"They will have to be put outside during the night. How heavy the scent! How many tons of it are there?"

"I will have them taken away. . . . What are you going to do, Camilla?"

"I am going to get up. . . . Yes, I can manage, thank you. See, it's all passed off, I only needed to get up . . . Yes, they

85

will have to be put outside. . . . But wherever? No, wait, I have a big flat of my own, in Ariosto Square. You can probably see it from here. . . ."

"It's already dark. The air, I think, is a little fresher."

"Why are there so few people about?"

"Sh! Every word can be heard."

    ·   ·   ·   ·

"What are they talking about?"

"I don't know, Camilla. I think they are students. Boasting of some sort. Perhaps of the same thing as ourselves. . . ."

"Do let me go! They've stopped at the corner there! Heavens, he's tossed that little fellow over his head! Now it's all quiet again. How eerily the light does cling to the tree-tops! And no street-lamp to be seen. Are we not on the top one?"

"What's that, Camilla?"

"Is there another floor above us?"

"Yes, I think there is."

Camilla thrust her head out of the little window and her eye followed the overhanging raceme up to its branch.

"No. . . ." But Heine tried to stop her. "There isn't," she repeated, as she broke away from him.

"What are you getting at?"

"I had the impression that somebody was standing there, with a lamp at the window, crumbling the leaves and the shadows and throwing them out into the street, and I wanted to hold up my face, so that they fell on my cheeks. But there really is nobody there."

"But this is real poetry, Camilla!"

"Really? I cannot say. There—standing there—over there—near the theatre. Where that lilac-hued glow is."

"Who is standing there, Camilla?"

"You funny boy! Not *who*, but my house, of course."

"Yes. But these are whims. . . . If we could but somehow arrange . . ."

"A room has been booked for you."

"Really? How thoughtful! At last! What is the time? Let

us be going. Let us go and see what sort of a room I've got.
I'd love to see."

They left No. 8, both smiling and excited as schoolchildren
besieging Troy in a timber yard.

VII

Quite a long time before it broke, the Catholic church bells,
bowing frigidly all about them, in bursts of sudden clanging
from tumbling belfry beams, loquaciously began to herald the
approach of the new day. In the inn only one small lamp was
alight, and when the telephone bell, suddenly strident, rang,
this flared up, not to be dimmed again after. And was witness
to the night porter's scurrying across the hall to the telephone
and after a brief argument with the caller replacing the
receiver and vanishing down a dark corridor, only to reappear
a short time after, surfacing from the same bosom of twilight.

"Yes, the gentleman is leaving this morning, he will call you
back, if it is so urgent. In half an hour's time. Please let me
have your number. Whom are we to ask for?"

The little lamp burned on, even when, buttoning his clothes
as he went, with night-time, tiptoe gait, called to the telephone,
the occupant of No. 8 emerged from the side corridor into the
main one.

The little lamp happened to be exactly opposite the door of
that room, but in spite of that to get to the telephone the man
from No. 8 went for a corridor walk, and the first part of
that expedition lay somewhere in the region of the eighties.
After a brief interchange with the night porter, whose face
changed its expression at once, the anxious excitement giving
way to sudden lack of concern plus curiosity, he boldly took
up the receiver and after the usual formalities established
contact with his correspondent, in the form of the editor of
Voce.

"I must say, this is impious! Who told you I suffer from
insomnia?"

.   .   .   .   .

"Haven't you taken the telephone by mistake? You need the church tower! What's the great news? Come on, what is it?"

.　　　　.　　　　.　　　　.

"Yes, I have stayed on one day longer."

.　　　　.　　　　.　　　　.

"Yes, the hotel is quite right, I have not given them my home address and I do not intend to."

.　　　　.　　　　.　　　　.

"You? No, you shall not have it, either. No, I have never for a moment contemplated publishing it, let alone today, as you seem to have got into your head."

.　　　　.　　　　.　　　　.

"You cannot possibly ever need it."

.　　　　.　　　　.　　　　.

"My dear sir, please do not get excited. Altogether, the calmer you remain, the better. It will not even occur to Relinquimini to seek your intervention."

.　　　　.　　　　.　　　　.

"Because he has no need for it."

.　　　　.　　　　.　　　　.

"Once again let me point out how much I would value a little calmness on your part. Relinquimini never lost any sort of diary."

.　　　　.　　　　.　　　　.

"Look here!—though this is the first unambiguous thing you have said. . . . No, one hundred per cent: no!"

.　　　　.　　　　.　　　　.

"Again? Very well, if you like. But this is blackmail. Only within the limits of yesterday evening's issue of your *Voce*— which is far from being the same thing farther afield."

.　　　　.　　　　.　　　　.

"Since yesterday evening. Since six p.m."

.　　　　.　　　　.　　　　.

"Had you but indirectly got a whiff of what has frothed up on the yeast of that invention, you would look around for a rather sharper name for it, and it would be still farther from the truth than what you have just suggested to me."

.　　　　.　　　　.　　　　.

88

"Willingly. With pleasure. I can see no obstacles today . . . Heinrich Heine."

.　　　　.　　　　.　　　　.

"Precisely that."

.　　　　.　　　　.　　　　.

"I am most flattered to hear it."

.　　　　.　　　　.　　　　.

"You don't say so!"

.　　　　.　　　　.　　　　.

"Very glad to. How are we to achieve that? I am sorry, I really must travel today. Come down to the station, we can spend a moment together."

.　　　　.　　　　.　　　　.

"Nine thirty-five. Though all time is a concatenation of surprises. I don't think you had better come."

.　　　　.　　　　.　　　　.

"Come to the *albergo*. In the afternoon. That will be more certain. Or come and see me at the flat. In the evening. Tails, please. And flowers."

.　　　　.　　　　.　　　　.

"Yes. Yes, my dear sir, you are quite a Delphic figure."

.　　　　.　　　　.　　　　.

"Then tomorrow, on some duelling ground, outside the city."

.　　　　.　　　　.　　　　.

"Hm! But . . . perhaps I am not joking."

.　　　　.　　　　.　　　　.

"Or, if you're busy, both today and tomorrow. All day. Come—yes, look here, come to *Campo Santo* the day after tomorrow."

.　　　　.　　　　.　　　　.

"You think so?"

.　　　　.　　　　.　　　　.

"You think so?"

.　　　　.　　　　.　　　　.

"What a strange conversation, neither real daylight nor twilight. Well, good-bye now. I'm tired. I want to get back to my room."

.　　　　.　　　　.　　　　.

"I didn't quite catch? To room number eight? Oh, why yes. Yes, yes, number eight. It's a long room, my dear sir, with a very special climate inside. For five hours now it has been eternal Spring time. Good morning to you, sir!"

Mechanically, Heine whirled the handle, to cut the line.

"Don't put the light out, Enrico," came a voice from the depths of the corridor.

"Is that you, Camilla?"

Letters from Tula

I

IN the open the skylarks were pouring forth their song while
in a train on its way from Moscow the panting sun was
carried on many a striped, upholstered seat. And the sun was
setting. A bridge with the inscription *R. Upa* flowed past the
hundred windows at the same instant as the city swiftly
rushing out to meet it disclosed itself to the fireman flying
ahead of the train on the tender in the roar of his own shock
head of hair and the freshness of the evening excitement.

In the same instant, people who met in the streets were
bidding each other a good evening. To this some added:

"Have you been?"

The others answered:

"Just going."

This brought the reply:

"You're late. It's all over."

.   .   .   .   .

Tula, 10 p.m.

"So you changed over, as we fixed with the conductor. Just
now the General, when he vacated his place and went to
the bar, nodded to me as if we were old friends. The next
train Moscow way will be the 3 a.m. He was bidding me
good-bye, as he left. The porter opened the door for him. I
could hear the cabbies outside. Like sparrows, from a distance.
Darling, it was awful, seeing you off. Now you're gone, it's ten
times worse. No curb now on my imagination. It will fret me to
death. A tram's just coming. They're switching it over now. I

shall go and have a look at the town. What yearning! If only I could crush it, stifle it. It's so fierce. I shall write and write. My verse."

· · · · ·

Tula

"Oh, there's no middle way. At the second bell one should turn and go. Or else get into the train with the person one's seeing off, and go to the very end, to the grave. Think, it will be getting light when I do the whole journey back, stage by stage, in reverse, in every detail too, even the smallest. And all will then be fine points of exquisite torture.

"What a misfortune, to be born a poet! What a torturer imagination is! Sunshine—in a bottle of beer. A sediment on the very bottom of the bottle. Opposite me at my table there's a farm bailiff or something of the sort. Ruddy-faced. Stirring his coffee with green fingers. Oh, darling girl, I am surrounded by strangers. There was one witness, now gone (the General). There is one other—that magistrate—they won't recognize me. Mean minds. The creatures think they can lap up their sunshine, out of a saucer with their milk. They think their flies don't drown in yours, the cooks' pans clatter, the soda-water hisses and the coppers chink on the marble as if they had their own language. I'm going to stroll round and have a look at the town. Some distance from the station. There is a tram, but not worth it. About forty minutes walk, I'm told. Found that receipt, you were right. Will hardly manage it tomorrow, shall need a good sleep. The day after. But don't you worry, it's the public pawnbroker, there's time. Oh, writing is just self-torture. Yet I can't bring myself to part entirely from you."

· · · · ·

Five hours went by. The silence was striking. It became impossible to distinguish where herbage ended, coal began. A star twinkled. Not another living soul at the hydrant. The water in the wooden tank was black. On the surface quivered the reflection of a birch-tree. Feverish. But was very distant, that. Very, very distant. That birch-tree was the only soul on the road.

The silence was exceptionally dense. On the flat earth lay boilers and trucks, and no breath in them. They were like low storm clouds gathering on a windless night. Were it not April, there would be streak lightning. Yet the sky was uneasy. Overcome by the transparency, as if by a sickness, stirred from within too, by Spring, uneasy. The last coach of the Tula trams came in from the town. The wooden tip-over backs of the seats clattered. The last to emerge was a man with a lot of letters sticking out of the broad pockets of his loose-cut overcoat. The rest went straight into the waiting-room and made for a party of very peculiar young people noisily having supper at the far end. But the newcomer stayed this side of the façade, looking for the green blotch of a letter-box. But it was impossible to say where the herbage ended and the coal began, and when the sluggish vapour dragged the shaft over the turf and this ploughed its iron tip into the path, no dust at all rose, it was only by the lantern hanging outside the stables that he knew at all. The night then emitted a drawn-out, throaty sound. After that, all was utterly still, very, very far away, beyond the horizon.

.　　.　　.　　.　　.

Tula, 10 (*crossed out*) 11 *p.m.*
"Dear one, check in your textbook. You've got Kluchevski with you, I put it in the trunk myself. I don't know how to begin. I still can't grasp this. It's so strange. So terrible too. While I write these words, everything is going on as usual on the other side of the table. All being so clever, making speeches, tossing fine words to and fro, dramatically wiping their clean-shaven mugs, then planting their napkins demonstratively on the table. I've not explained who. The worst sort of bohemians. (Carefully crossed out.) A film-making company from Moscow. Been shooting *Ivan the Terrible etcetera*—shots in the Kremlin and anywhere else they had ramparts.

93

"Read what Kluchevski has to say.about it—I've not read it myself, but think he's surely described the business about Bolotnikov (Pyotr). Anyway, that's what had brought them out to the Upa. Learned that they've dotted the i and shot from the far bank. Now their seventeenth century's all tucked away in their trunks, and all the rest can sprawl over a dirty tablecloth. Polish women are frightful, but scions of true Russian blue-blood a damn sight worse.

"Dearest person! It makes me want to puke. An exhibition of the ideals of our age. The foul fumes they produce, well, we're all of us responsible. Poisonous fug of boorishness and the most miserable, vulgar arrogance. Myself. Darling, I've already dropped two letters. Don't recall what I said. Here's the vocabulary of those (crossed out, rejected without substitution). Here's their vocabulary: genius, poet, fed-up, verse, nothing in him (or her) drama, woman, I—and she. How frightful to see oneself in others. All a caricature on . . . (not completed).

2 o'clock

"The heart's faith's greater than ever, I swear to you, the time will come—no, first let me tell you: torment, torment me night, not finished yet, scorch to the ground, burn, burn clear and bright, force your way through the rubble piled in, through the forgotten, furious, fiery word 'conscience'. (This underlined, the pen in places tearing through the paper.) Oh blaze, you furious crude oil tongue of flame, lighting the floor of the night.

"That's the sort of shape life's taken on our earth, ever since the world lost any points at which a man might warm his soul with the fire of shame; shame, universally, now sodden, refuses to burn at all. Lies, and chaotic loss of clear ways. It began thirty years ago, since when any a bit out of the usual run, old or young, spend their whole lives damping down shame. Now it has spread to the whole world, even the utterly unknown. For the first, for the very first time since remotest childhood fire is consuming me (all crossed out)."

A fresh attempt. The letter is never sent.

"How describe it to you? I shall have to start from the end.
Or it won't work. Right—only let me put it in the third person.
I did write about the individual who went strolling past the
luggage platform, didn't I? Right, then. A poet, from now on
indicated by that designation, till fire purges him, a poet in
inverted commas, a 'poet,' that is, observes himself in a party
of actors letting rip on a stage revelative of the comrades and
the age alike. Is he just playing about? No. He's assured the
identification is no chimera. They get up and approach him.
Call him 'colleague', just to ask if he's got small change for a
three-rouble piece. He disseminates the illusion. It isn't only
actors who shave. Produces three roubles' worth of twenty-
copeck pieces. Marks himself off from the actor. Not the shaved
physiognomies that matter. It was that word *colleague* on the
lips of such rats. Indeed. And he was right. Practical mani-
festation of the indictment. At the same moment something
new happened, merest trifle, in its own way shattering to all
taking place or gone through in that restaurant up to that
moment.

"The 'poet' recognized the man walking up and down in the
luggage hall. Seen his face somewhere, some time. Somewhere
local. Not once only, not today, or merely a particular day,
but various moments, in various places. When they made up
that special train, for instance, at Astapovo, with a luggage
wagon as tomb, and the crowd of unknowns were all leaving
the station in a variety of trains, which were all criss-crossing
and trying to link up one with another all day long because of
the unforeseen events at that complicated junction where four
main lines came together and intercrossed and turned back
again and went their ways.

"Here in a flash, realization seizes on all that happened to
the 'poet' in the restaurant, like a lever switching to another
scene, as follows: of course, it was Tula! Of course, it was night.
Night-time at Tula. Night in passages of the Tolstoy story.
Was it astonishing if the compass needles began to hop about?
What happened was in the nature of the place. It was an event
on the *territory of conscience*, its lodestone-bearing, gravity-

making part. That's the end of the 'poet'. He swears it to you. He swears to you that some day, when he sees *Ivan the Terrible* on the screen (after all, that will in due course come about) the sequence on the Upa will leave him utterly isolated, unless by then the actors mend their ways, unless some day they can spend a whole day dancing about on a mine-sown territory of the spirit and yet remain untouched in their boorishness and boasting, dreamers in every sense."

While these lines were being penned, lights appeared from huts, low-down, at sleeper level, and wound their way along the tracks. Whistles sounded. Cast iron was awakened, twisted chains cried out. Past the loading ramp slowly slipped the coaches. Had long been slipping, goods trucks without end. And behind them, looming larger, the approach of something that breathed hard, an unknown night creature. Because crash after crash in the trail of the locomotive suddenly approaching came a clearing of tracks, the unexpected advent of night within the horizon of the empty loading ramp, the advent of silence throughout the world of signals and stars—the oncoming of peace in the open country. And in this moment of time there was a hoarse breathing behind the goods train, ever nearer, sliding up, under the station roofing.

While these lines were being written, they had begun to make up the mixed goods-and-passenger to Yeletzk.

The writer had come out on to the platform. It was night, throughout the vast marsh of the Russian conscience. Night illuminated by lanterns. Through it, the rails bending under them, slowly crept open trucks with winnowing gear under canvas. The shadows trampled down the night, silencing the tufty steam breaking like barn-door cocks from the valves. The writer came round the far side of the station. Beyond the façade.

While those lines were penned, nothing had changed, throughout the spaces of conscience. From it all rose a reek of mould and mud. In the far distance, hazily showing, a birch-tree, and the outline of the water tank, fallen pearl in a sea of mud. Strips of light broke from the restaurant into the free air and fell on the floor of the tram-car, beneath the seats.

They grew turbulent, in their wake the clash of beer and folly and foul smells, splashing with the light under the seats. And when the station windows died down, somewhere close could be heard hoarse breath and snoring. He had by now forgotten with whom he had travelled here, to whom he had bid farewell, to whom he had been writing. It seemed to him now that everything would begin again from the point at which he ceased to hear himself. And there was at last complete, physical silence in his soul. Not an Ibsen silence, but an *acoustical* silence.

So he thought. Then a shudder passed through his body. The east turned grey, and hurried, flustered dew settled on all the face of conscience deep engulfed still in profoundest night. It was time to think about his ticket. The cocks were crowing, and there was somebody in the ticket office.

II

Only then, at last, in the town, an extremely strange elderly man prepared for bed in an inn in Posolskaya Street. While letters were being written at the station, that hotel room shivered from feathered footsteps, and the candle in the window caught a whisper frequently broken by silence. It was not the voice of the elderly man, although there was nobody else but him in the room. All this was most peculiar.

The elderly man had spent a most unusual day. As soon as he had found out that it was no play, but for the time being no more than free flight of fancy which would only turn into a play when shown at the *Chary*, he turned away most disappointed. At first sight of those medieval nobles and *voyvodes* milling about on the far shore and a crowd of common folk involving chain-mail headpieces knocked off their heads into the nettles, at sight of those Poles hanging on to the laburnums on the cliff face and their battle-axes so unresponsive to the sunshine and so unringing, the elderly man had begun rummaging in his own repertoire. But found no such chronicle there. And then decided this must be before his

97

period, it was Ozerov or Sumarokov, at which point somebody
pointed out the cameraman to him and by mentioning the
Chary picture-house, an institution which he heartily detested,
reminded him that he was old and isolated in a new age. And
he went on his way, most depressed.

On he trudged in his well-worn nankeen trousers and
reflected that now there was nobody left who would call him
Sava old man. It was a festive sort of day. Scattered debris of
sunflower seeds. He basked in it. Spitting and dribbling a
collar of husks, through throaty mutter, new speech in old.
High up the spongy roll of the melting moon. Cold-seeming
sky, amazed to be so distant. Voices fruity by food and drink
consumed. That chantarelle, that rye round loaf, that smoked
fat bacon and that vodka soaked even into the echo which
heady swam beyond the river. In other streets were crowds,
pock-marked the skirts and women too with clumsy pleats.

And dogged their steps close-heeled the tall steppe-grass.
Soft rose the mist of dust, eyelids were glued, the burdock
palms to silt, in whorls the wattle through, to girls' frocks
clinging close. His walking-stick perceived the fragmented
sclerotics of his age. And on that extension of his now knotted
fibres leant his spasmodic, grown cautious gouty frame.

. . . . .

All that day he had had the feeling of being mixed up in
crowds which were excessively noisy. The consequence, of
course, of the sight he had seen. Which left his need for
dramatic human speech unrequited. And that untalkative
blankness rang in the old man's ears.

All the day he had felt ill since from that far bank he had
not heard a single pentameter.

And when night came at last, sat down at a table, propped
head on hand and deep sank into thought. And decided this
was the end of him. So unlike his recent years, unwavering
bitter as they were, was this soul turmoil. And resolved to take
his decorations out of the cupboard and warn somebody, were
it only the man at the door (no matter whom), but instead

sat on, waiting to see, perhaps it was only a passing mood, it would pass.

Past him, shadow-sly, the tram bobbed by. The last tram to the station.

A half hour since. The star gleamed bright. No other soul in sight. Quite late, now, it was. A candle, guttering, flickering faint. And the outlines of the shelving shimmered to life and soft subsided to four streams of blackness. Far off, far off. Outside, a door banged, soft and excited, voices sprang up, seemly on such a night of spring, with not a soul about, only overhead, one lighted room, one open casement.

The ageing man stood up. Transformed. At last! And time too! Found—her and himself! Helped to it. And hastened to lend his hand to those hints, to let not one slip from him, to soak himself in them. And then relax. With a few steps he reached the door, eyes half closed, waving one hand, the other on his chin. Recalling. And all at once stood erect and cheerfully strolled back, with gait not his, another's. Clearly acting a part.

.   .   .   .   .

"What a hurricane, oh, what a hurricane, my dear Liubov Petrovna," he declared.

Then cleared his throat, and spat into his handkerchief. And again:

"What a hurricane, oh, what a hurricane it is, my dear girl!"

And this time did not cough. And it sounded more real.

He began to wave his arms and whirl about, as if coming in from a storm, shaking off the snow, taking off his fur coat. For a few moments he waited, to see what answer would come from the other side of the dividing wall, then, as if unable to wait, still in that stranger voice, demanded:

"Aren't you there, Liubov Petrovna?" and started violently when, *as was only to be expected,* from beyond that dividing wall—two and a half tens of years away—he heard the cheerful response: "Yes, I'm here."

99

Then, again, this time more himself, with self-deception which would have been the pride of any counterpart of himself in such position, reaching out towards the wall oh so fumblingly, with eyes askance and words disjointed all, mumbled:

"Er . . . er . . . worry . . . Liubov Petrovna. . . . I suppose . . . Sava Ignatievich is not there?"

That, now, was the utter limit. Beyond. Seeing them both. Her and himself. Then, old man, with silent sobbing choked. And ticking clock. Weeping and whispering both. The silence so unusual. While, shuddering, senile, helplessly holding handkerchief to eyes and cheeks, as he shivered he crushed the rag, shaking his head and thrusting away the truth, as if giggling, yet gasping aghast with surprise that still, God forgive, he was he and not torn asunder—on the tracks of cast steel for the mixed goods-and-passenger to Yeletzk to try to pick up.

.   .   .   .   .

For a whole hour, as in alcohol in a jar, he preserved his youth, then, when the last tear dried away, all had collapsed, all borne away, all for ever gone. At once his substance dulled, dust settled in and on. And then, at last with heavy sigh, humble in guilt, he yawned and prepared for bed.

.   .   .   .   .

He also shaved his moustache, as in the story too. And also, as principal person, sought physical silence. In the story solely he too found it, by making a stranger speak through his lips.

.   .   .   .   .

The Moscow train rolled on, its freight, on so many slumbering bodies, an immense crimson sun. This very minute risen above the swelling land and rising high.

To Mikhail Alekseyevich Kuzmin, 1924

Aerial Routes

I

PROPPING her back against the trunk, the nurse slept on under the ancient mulberry. When an enormous purple cloud rose up at the road edge, silencing even the crickets that made such sultry crackling music in the grass and in the camps the sigh of the drums finally snapped off the end, the earth's eyes dimmed, and life ceased in the world.

"Coom on! Coom on!" harelipped she yelled, the half-wit cow-girl, dragging her crushed foot in front of the steer, and, brandishing a wild branch like a lightning flash, appeared in a cloud of rubbish from the far side of the orchard, where all wild growth began, nightshades and bricks, crumpled wire and mouldy dankness.

Then vanished.

The storm-cloud swept its eye over the close-cut, scorched stubbles. Which stretched to the very skyline. Reared lightly up. The storm-cloud. The stubbles stretched farther still, even beyond the camps. Sank back to fore-feet, the storm-cloud, glided across the road, and noiselessly slipped away along the fourth rail of the railway track. And the bushes all bared their heads down the slopes of the cutting and followed after. Flowed on, bowing to the cloud. And the cloud made no answer.

From the tree the mulberries dropped. And caterpillars. Plague-stricken by heat they fell from their twigs and plopped into nurse's apron—and they ceased to think at all.

The child now crawled to the water-tap. He had been crawling for some time. He crawled on farther.

101

When, at last, it pours out, and both pairs of rails fly off down the leaning wattle fences, in flight from the black, watery night now lowered on to them. When, foaming and feeling its way, the water as it races by will cry out to you not to be afraid of it, it is called downpour and love and something else too, I will relate how as the sun went down the parents of the little boy kidnapped cleaned their white canvas shoes and it was very early when, snow-white, as for a round of tennis, they went through the still, dark garden and came out by the post which shows the way to the station at the very moment when the fat-bellied disc of the boiler, rolling cautious from behind the market-gardens, enveloped the Turkish confectioner's in clouds of short-breathed yellow smoke.

They were going down to the harbour to meet the midshipman who once had loved her and had been her husband's great friend and this morning after a round-the-world instructional voyage was expected to reach their town. And her husband was burning with impatience, anxious as soon as ever possible to initiate his friend into the profound significance of the fatherhood of which he still had not quite had enough. That's how things were. That so simple event struck you as if almost the very first case of the magic of its primeval significance. It was so new for you that, look! there could even be a man who had been all round the world and seen his fill of everything and, one might think, really had something to talk about, yet it seemed to you that when you at last did meet him it was he who would be audience while you staggered his comprehension with your rattle.

The very opposite of her husband, she—as the anchor is to the waves—was drawn by the metallic clank and clamour of the harbour, by the brownish rust of those three-funnel giants, by the grain in streams out-pouring, under the bright splashing of skies and sails and sailor-boys. Their urges did not match at all.

It was raining, pouring buckets—I am coming to the promised story. Above the ditch creaked the hazel tops. Across the open ground scurried two human shapes. The man had a black beard. The woman's shaggy mane followed free, wind-swept. The man was wearing a green caftan and silver ear-rings. In his arms he held an ecstatic child. And it poured and poured, buckets.

II

It turned out that he had long since been granted his commission. Eleven p.m. The last train from the town came rolling into the station. It had just wept and wailed its fill, and now, as the journey rounded off, it grew more cheerful, even burst into laughter. It filled full lungs at last with the whole district, with the leaves, sand and dew pouring into its bursting reservoirs, it halted, clapped its hands and was suddenly silent awaiting a howl of response. From all tracks the echoes should rally. When it heard this, the lady, the sailor and the civilian all in white would turn off the road on to the footpath and straight in front of them, from behind the poplars, out would float the dazzling disc of the dew-lapped roof. They would follow the path, to the hedge, bang the wicket to, and without letting fall a drop from its ridges, cornices, gutters, tickling the ear-rings that danced in her ears, the galvanized planet would begin to roll up to meet them. The rumble of the train rolling away would then suddenly break out again, far away, before crumbling to a rain of tiny, dying soapsuds. Then indeed it would seem not to be a train at all, but water rockets with which the sea was having great fun. Beyond the station wood the moon would climb up on to the road. And then, looking back at the whole scene, you would get the impression that an ever forgetful poet you knew so well had made it all up, and now it would even be a thing for Christmas stockings. You will recall that some time past you saw that same fence in your sleep, and then it was called the edge of the world.

On the moon-bathed porch a bucket of lime-wash showed white. Brush uppermost, a painter's broom lay propped against the wall. Then a window was opened, overlooking the garden.

"They've been liming today," came the woman's quiet voice. "Smell it? Let's go and have supper."

And again there was silence. But it did not last long. There was a sudden hubbub in the house.

"What? What do you mean, not there? He's lost?"

It was a bass voice hoarse as a slackened string and a woman's contralto voice glittering with hysteria, crying together.

"Under the tree? Under the tree? Let her get up this instant and tell us what's happened. And do stop that howling! For Christ's sake don't hang on to my arms like that! God Almighty, what on earth is the woman thinking of? Tosha! Tosha darling, Tosha, Tosha! How dare you! How dare you! To my face! You shameless, shameful slattern!"

The words ceased to be words, ran wretchedly together. Broke off. Faded far. Then were no longer to be heard.

The night was ending. But it was still far to dawn. The world was stacked with silence-shattered shapes. Like stooked corn. Resting. As day approached, the distances between the shapes increased, just as if they could thus rest better. They parted, they receded. In the gaps between them inaudibly the chilling meads under their sweat-soaked saddle-cloths puffed and whinnied one to another! Rarely did any shape turn out to be a tree, a cloud or other familiar object. Most were vague, anonymous heaps. They were slightly dizzy, and in that half-fainting state they could scarcely have said whether or not there had just been a shower and it had stopped, or there was about to be one, it would begin to spatter its first drops any moment. Tipping and dipping, they were constantly shuttled from past to future and from future to past. Like sand in quickly turning hour-glasses.

But, a far flight from then, like linen torn by a gust of wind at daybreak and carried who knew whither, on the farther edge of the fields three human shapes now showed, while on the opposite side from them eternally murmured and reverberated the ever-nascent mutter of the distant sea. But these four persons were borne solely from past into future, and never reversed. The human beings in white scurried from place to place, constantly bending down and straightening their backs again, leaping over ditches. Hidden for a moment, they would reappear at some entirely different point of the field boundary. Though a long way one from another, they kept shouting, waving across one to the other, and as their signs were always misinterpreted, immediately had to start signalling anew, more jerkily and more angrily and often, to show that the messages had not been understood, they changed places. And then, not to go back on their tracks, each went on searching where the other had left off. The united vigour which those figures manifested left the impression of people who the night before had decided to play tennis, but lost their ball and now were fudging all the ditches for it, and when they found it would start all over again.

There was not a breath of wind to stir the shapes which had been resting, yet it was easy to surmise that daybreak was already at hand, and when one looked at those people flitting about over the countryside like spasmodic whirlwinds, one might well have thought that the fields had been lashed and churned up by wind and darkness and fear as some black, broken, three-toothed comb harrowed and harried the world.

There is a law by which nothing can ever happen to ourselves that close at hand is bound to happen to others. Writers have more than once quoted this rule. Its incontrovertibility is to be seen in the fact that while our friends are still getting to know us, we perhaps consider a misfortune is reparable. But by the time we are finally convinced that it is not, our friends have ceased to try to know us, and, as if to confirm the law, we ourselves become different, that is, we ourselves are the ones called upon to burn and to be ruined, brought to court or clapped in the madhouse.

So long as still healthy, these people nagged at the nurse, it surely seemed to them that they would by sheer reason of their anger with the woman afterwards be able just to go into the nursery and there with sighs of relief find their little boy established where he should be in precise ratio to the degree of their alarm and their rage. But when they went, the sight of the empty cot stripped the skin from their voices. But even with soul thus flayed, rushing out, to search, first in the garden, then fanning farther and farther beyond in their quest,

105

for a considerable time they were still creatures of our own decade. That is to say, they still sought solely that they might find. But gradually, as the hours crept by, as the very night changed face, they too changed. And now, as that night came to its end, they were quite unrecognizable people, no longer understood by what fault of theirs or to what purpose cruel space thus gave them no respite, but continued to drag them and to toss them to all the four quarters of that vast world in which their little child would never more be seen. And had long forgotten the midshipman, who had crossed to search below the cliffs.

Is it by reason of this dubious observation that the author has been concealing from his readers what he knows so very well? For does he not know better than anyone else that the moment in the hamlet the bakers' shops took down their shutters and the first trains scattered wide, news of the sad event flashed from villa to villa and at last informed twin Olginaya schoolboys where they might at last deliver their little anonymous friend, trophy of yesterday's triumph.

.　　.　　.　　.　　.

From under the trees and under felt hats low set on foreheads there broke at last the first beginnings of morning still not fully conscious. Day broke in stages, with intervals. Suddenly the murmur of the sea had seemed no more and everything was even stiller than before. Coming from who knew tell where, a sweetish, repetitive effervescence pervaded the tree-tops. One by one, as with sweating silver their lattice lapped the fences, they long sank back to slumber rudely broken. Smooth and detached, two rare diamonds twinkled in the deep nests of that blissful half-light—a bird and its twittering song. Alarmed by its loneliness and abashed by its negligibility, the little songster passionately strove without trace to become merged in that endless ocean of dew incapable of mastering its own thoughts, so distracted and drowsy it was. And succeeded. Its head cocked on one side and its eyes tightly closed, it soundlessly dissolved into the silliness and the sadness of this world now newly born, and rejoiced in its own disappearance. But lacked the strength. Then, all at once, breaking through its resistance and revealing its peeping up head with unattainable grace at unattainable height like a planet of ice, its powerful trilling glittered, its springy tattoo far-scattering in needle-fine spokes, so its sprinkling trilling rang clear and froze in amazement as if splashed on a dish with one huge marvelling eye.

But now the world all at once began to grow lighter in a more concerted way. The garden filled to the brim with moist, white light, light which clung most closely to the stuccoed wall, to the gravelled paths and the trunks of those fruit trees which had been smeared with a coppery wash now whitish like lime. It was now, with as death-like an expression on her face, that the mother of the child came dragging her feet in from the fields. Without pause, with stumbling steps, she cut straight across the garden towards the back of the house, indifferent to where she trod or into what her feet might sink. The garden beds tossed her up and let her subside again as if her anxiety were in need of such fresh agitation. And when she had crossed the orchard, she came near that part of the fence from which could be seen the road to the camps. And the midshipman was just making for this point, and proposing to climb over the fence, not to have to go all round the garden. Yawning, the eastern sky bore him up on to the fence like the white sail of a heeled-over yawl. And she awaited him, holding on to the fencing cross-rails. It was clear, she was going to make a pronouncement and her succinct words were prepared.

.   .   .   .   .

The same proximity of shower just over or about to be was to be felt down on the sea-shore as up on the cliff. Whence could that murmur come, audible all night on the other side of the canvas? The sea now lay cooling, like the silvered back of a mirror, only its shore fringe faintly gasping and whimpering, the horizon now sickly yellow and morose. Forgivable in a dawn pressed to the rear wall of a huge pigsty full-mucked

107

for hundreds of miles, where at any moment from all sides the
frenzied flood might surge. For the moment they crept on their
bellies, scarce perceptibly nudging each other, an innumerable
herd as it were of slimy black swine. Out on to the cliff—to
cliff-top had climbed the midshipman. With gait that was
nimble and glad. From stone to stone bounding. For as he had
reached the top he had learned a shattering piece of news.
From the sands picked a sea-smooth tile and level flicked it
out to the water. And as if spittle spattered it skimmed
swiftly low away with the same elusive young sound that all
shallow waters reveal. In the very last instant, when, utterly
frantic by failure, he had turned to go back to the villa.
And, as he had drawn near from the side of the common,
Lelia had rushed up to the fence from inside, was there to
await till he came, and then in quick rush of syllables gasped:
"We're—all in. . . . Save us. . . . You must find him . . . He's . . .
He's your son!"

Whereupon he seized her hand, and she tore herself away
and escaped. And when he climbed over into the garden, she
was now nowhere to be found. Again he picked up a stone.
And so, picking and throwing without cease, set out from the
house again, to vanish beyond the cliff edge. While behind him
his tracks lived on, never still. He, too, was dead tired. It was
the shingle, slipping and slithering, that sighed and uneasily
turned as he noisily edged himself in and got comfortable, to
sleep his ease at last, in utter peace.

III

More than fifteen years had passed. Outside, the light was
failing, indoors it was dark. A woman whom nobody knew
was enquiring for the third time for a member of the *Presidium*
of the *Provincial Executive Committee*, a former naval officer
named Polivanov. Facing her, a soldier, fed-up. Through the
hall window could be seen the yard: piles of bricks, snow-
covered. At the back of the yard, where once had been a
rubbish pit, now a long-neglected mountain of refuse, the sky

was a dreamy forestry commission plantation growing up the slopes of that accumulation of dead cats and empty food-tins resurrecting now in the thaw and clearing their throats and beginning to pant with former Springs and drip-dripping, sparrow rumour and chatter of plenty. Yet one only needed to take one's eyes from that backyard corner and peer up above to be amazed how utterly new the sky was.

The ability it now possessed all the clock round to sweep far to all sides from sea and from railroad head the thunder and mutter of rifles and guns, had thrust deep back its remembrance of 1905. Quite as if from end to end whirled away by the highroad roller in its heady cannonade and now finally slaughtered and by this in-trodden, it frowned, speechless, and without any movement led off from the scene as indeed in Winter is the nature of any ribbon of the monotonously unwinding trail of the rails.

What on earth had come over the sky? Even by day it suggested the image of night that we see in our youth and when marching far. Even after midday it was striking, infinitely outstanding, even after midday took its fill of the ravaged earth, overthrowing the sleepy and raising up dreamers.

These were the aerial routes by which daily, like trains, the through thoughts of Liebknecht, Lenin and a handful of minds of their flight of thought left the station. Those were the routes established on a level adequate for the passage of any frontiers, whatever their name. One of the lines, laid away back during the war, had maintained all the one-time strategical importance imposed on the engineers by the nature of the front above which they had had to construct it. This old military line, somewhere, at places of its own choosing and at hours of its own selection, cutting through the frontiers of Poland and then of Germany, here, at its very beginning, before everybody's eyes, burst from the limits of understanding of indirectness and its patience. It passed over the yard of this house, and the yard was fearsome of the far-offness of the ultimate destination and the oppressive clumsiness of the route, as a fugitive suburb is ever afraid of the railway line that misses it far.

The soldier's reply to the lady was that Polivanov had not yet returned. Three species of fed-upness rang in his voice. There was the fed-upness of a creature accustomed to liquid mud suddenly finding itself in dry dust. There was the fed-upness of a man routined in sequestering and requisitioning detachments in which it had been he who put the questions and a dame like this made the answers, therefore fed-up that the proper order of model duologue should thus be broken and topsy-turveyed. Finally there was the imaginary fed-upness with which any intrusion of the most everyday substance endows anything utterly unheard-of. And, being perfectly well aware how utterly unheard-of the set-up of recent times must seem to this lady, the soldier became deliberately obstructive, as if utterly unaware what her feelings might be, and never in his whole life had he breathed aught but the good atmosphere of dictatorship. All at once, in came darling Lyov. Say: a shoulder strap of behemothean footsteps at one fell swoop swept him with cold fresh breath of snow, and silence unhallowed, straight in from mid-air to the second floor. Snatching at the object, which transpired to be a brief-case, the soldier halted the incomer much as one might a fair in full swing.

"Just think"—he addressed him—"somebody's been round from *Prisoners and Booty HQ*."

"About those Hungarians again?"

"Of course."

"But they've had their answer flat. No papers, no departure!"

"And what did I say? It's very clear to me it's because of the ships. And that's how I put it to them."

"And what did they say then?"

"They knew all that without us. It's up to you to see the papers are in order. As if as crew. Once there, so to speak, all's in order. Make room for others."

"Right. And what else?"

"Nothing more. All they're worried about is the permit. The order, they say."

"But of course not," Polivanov interrupted. "Why go on repeating? I wasn't talking about that!"

"There's a despatch in from Kanatnaya," the soldier went on, mentioning the street where the Extraordinary Commission had its HQ. Then, drawing closer, he lowered his voice to a whisper, as if giving secret instructions.

"You don't mean it? So that's how it stands, is it? Impossible!" Polivanov objected, but distracted and rather unconcerned.

The soldier fell back. For a moment the two men stood, without a word being spoken.

"Brought the bread?" the soldier then asked, all at once, and morosely, for the bulging brief-case might well have served an answer. 'Oh yes, there is something else. A citizeness to see you."

"Right. Right. Right," drawled Polivanov, still very distracted.

The hawser of giant footsteps drew tight, quivering. The portfolio came to life.

"In my office, Comrade," he said coldly to the lady in question.

He had not recognized her.

In comparison with the vestibule, the office was pitch dark. She followed him in. Once across the threshold, she halted. No doubt the room was carpeted, for he had not taken two or at most three paces when he seemed to vanish. Then similar footsteps sounded at the far end of that murk. There came sounds as of systematic clearing of the top of a desk, glasses being moved, crumbs, lumps of sugar, parts of a stripped down revolver, hexagonal pencils.

Carefully he drew his hand across the desk, tipping something over, wiping something as he fumbled for matches. Imagination had only just transported that room with its pictures on the bookshelf-lined walls, its palms and its bronzes, to a boulevard of onetime Petersburg and a standard lamp with a whole handful of lights in an outstretched hand to take them riding down the whole boulevard, when suddenly the telephone rang. That jingling bell with field post or hamlet at the other end was an instant reminder of the wire feeling its way out from this place through a town engulfed in utter

111

darkness and of the fact that the action was taking place out in the country, under the bolsheviks.

"Yes," replied the dissatisfied, impatient and dead-tired man, and no doubt shielded his eyes with his hand. "Yes. I am aware of it. I am aware of it. Nonsense. Check all along the line. Nonsense. I have been in touch with HQ. I've been able to get Zhmerinka for the past hour. And is that all? Yes, I will, I'll let you know. Why, of course not, in about twenty minutes! That all?"

"Well, Comrade, and what can I do for you?"—in one hand a matchbox, in the other a bluish spot of sputtering sulphurous flame, he addressed his visitor. And then, almost simultaneously with the sound of falling, scattering matches, rang out her glittering, shattering whisper.

"Lelia!" beside himself, cried Polivanov. "Impossible! Forgive me! Can it be? You, Lelia!"

"Yes . . . yes . . . how . . . ah! let me get my breath. . . . Thank God! I've found you!" she whispered, panting and crying at once.

.   .   .   .   .

Suddenly it all vanished. In the gleam of a lighted oil-glimmer, a man in a short unbuttoned tunic, corroded by acute lack of sleep, and a woman straight from the station, filthy. Long unwashed. Facing one another. In the glow of that oil-glimmer her coming, the death of Dmitri and of her little daughter, of the very existence of whom he had known nothing, and in short all she had managed to tell him before the lamp was alight, seemed depressingly just in its comprehensiveness, an open invitation to him who listened to plunge into his own grave too, in so far as his sympathy were not mere empty words. Then, with vision of her in that oil-glimmer, to his mind at once came all that past story by reason of which, meeting now, they had not fallen on each other's necks and kissed. And he could not but smile faintly as he marvelled at the vigour of such prejudices. In the light of the oil-glimmer all her hopes of the style of this office vanished.

112

For this man now seemed so alien to her that it was quite impossible to write off the feeling as a change. The more determinedly therefore did she proceed to her business, once again, as on that former occasion, hastening to say her say blindly, parrot-fashion, as if on an errand for another.

"If you care for our child. . . ."

That was her opening.

"Again?" Polivanov blazed out at once and began to talk and talk and talk, at top speed, never-halting. As if writing an article. With elaborate relative clauses. Stuffed with commas. Paced about the office, halting here, halting there, with wide gestures of helpless indignation, frenzied gestures of exasperation. And when he did interrupt himself it was only to frown and pluck at the skin over the bridge of his nose with thumb and two fingers, fretting and massaging that spot as the source of this indignation now beginning to gutter and dry up.

He implored her to stop thinking that other people were subject to her whims and she could twist everybody round her little finger. By all that was sacred he entreated her once and for all to abandon such fancy notions, particularly seeing how on that other occasion she had in the end had to confess how wrong she had been. He told her that even if he accepted the ridiculous suggestion she had mooted, she would thereby merely achieve the very opposite of what she wanted. It was impossible to convince anyone that something which was not a minute ago, then was suddenly there, was no find, but a loss. He called to mind the high degree of irresponsibility and liberty he had felt the moment he accepted her fairy story and how that very instant he lost any desire to go on fudging about in ditches and dykes, all he wanted to do was have a good bath.

"So that even supposing time to go into reverse," he said, in a would-be essay of bitter sarcasm, and once again he was to start searching for a member of her family, his only concern would be for her personally or for y or for z, nohow for himself or her ludicrous ideas. . . .

"Have you finished?" she demanded, having given him a

chance to blow off some steam. "You are right, I had forgotten what I said myself. Do you really not remember? Maybe it was mean and despicable. I was out of my mind from joy that the boy had been found. And so remarkably. Our boy. Oh, Lyov darling—to think, if you only knew what danger he is in now! I don't know where to begin. Let's start from the beginning. We have not seen each other since that day. You don't know him. He is so trusting. That will one day be his ruin. There is a scoundrel, an adventurer—though I know we should not judge our fellow-men—Neploshaev's his name . . . he and Tosha were in the *Corps des Pages* together. . . ."

At these words Polivanov, still pacing the office, was rooted to the spot. He had ceased to listen at all. For, in the midst of all her other flow of words, she had now uttered the very surname which only a moment ago the soldier had whispered to him. Polivanov was well acquainted with the case. It was hopeless for the accused. And there was only an hour to go.

"So he was acting under a pseudonym, was he?"

The colour left her cheeks when she heard that question. It meant that he knew more than she did, and the matter was more serious even than she had described. She now completely forgot in whose HQ she was, and, imagining that the real crime had been the use of a false name, began a hasty defence of her son from precisely the wrong angle.

"But, Lyov dear, he couldn't possibly have made a stand openly. Now, could he?"

Again when he grasped that her child might be concealed behind any one of the names familiar to him from official papers, he had ceased to hear her. And, standing at his desk, he rang up another office and made certain enquiries, moving now from one conversation to another, ever deeper and more darkly into the town and into the night, till before him lay unravelled the utter ruin contained in the last and definitely reliable information.

He turned his head. Lelia had gone. He was aware of a frightful aching in his eye-sockets and as his glance swept the room it swam before his vision, a confusion of stalactites and rivulets. He made to pucker the skin on the bridge of his nose, but instead he rubbed his eyes, and when he did so the stalactites danced and became misty. It would not have troubled him so much, had those spasms not been so frequent and so inaudible. Then he discovered her. Like an enormous, unbroken doll she lay between the block of his desk and the chair, on that same layer of shavings and rubbish which in the darkness, while still conscious, she had taken to be a rug.